RETURNING TO CLAIM HIS HEIR

AMANDA CINELLI

MILLS & BOON

First published in Great Britain 2021
by Mills & Boon, an imprint of HarperCollins*Publishers* Ltd,
1 London Bridge Street, London, SE1 9GF

www.harpercollins.co.uk

HarperCollins*Publishers*
1st Floor, Watermarque Building,
Ringsend Road, Dublin 4, Ireland

Large Print edition 2021

Returning to Claim His Heir © 2021 Amanda Cinelli

ISBN: 978-0-263-28858-2

05/21

MIX
Paper from
responsible sources
FSC™ C007454

This book is produced from independently certified FSC™ paper to ensure responsible forest management. For more information visit www.harpercollins.co.uk/green.

Printed and bound in Great Britain
by CPI Group (UK) Ltd, Croydon, CR0 4YY

For those who have grieved.
May the sun always shine after the storm.

CHAPTER ONE

IT WASN'T OFTEN that a man could say he'd looked upon his own grave. Duarte Avelar stood frozen in the sleepy English village graveyard, staring at the elegant family crypt where he and his twin sister had laid their beloved parents to rest seven years before.

But now a third name had been added to the marble plaque.

His own.

Dried wreaths and bouquets lined the resting place, with small notecards and offerings of condolences from friends and business colleagues alike. He'd been told his memorial service had been a grand affair, filled with Europe's wealthy elite, come to pay their respects to one of their favourite billionaire playboys.

His mind conjured up an image of his twin sister, Dani, accepting their sympathies, standing in this very spot to watch as they lowered an empty coffin into the ground…

His stomach lurched, nausea burning as he turned away and moved swiftly through the empty cemetery grounds. A sleek black car awaited him outside the gates, the young male chauffeur studiously staring at the wet ground as he held the door open. A pair of hulking bodyguards in plain clothes stood nearby, quietly focused on monitoring the surrounding countryside.

He had once enjoyed a certain level of familiarity with his staff. Had prided himself on being considered a likeable employer, easygoing and approachable. And yet for the past two weeks, since his shock return, he had been a pariah. It seemed everyone had been forewarned of his unpredictable temperament and had decided that ignoring him was the safest option.

Still, he caught them trying not to stare at the thick crosshatched scarring that spanned his face from the centre of his left eyebrow to the tip of his ear. He saw their stricken gazes upon seeing the scars along the rest of his torso when he went for his twice-daily swim.

He had gone from being the kind of man who could command a boardroom and charm any woman in his path to being one who avoided his own staff so as not to make them nervous.

His sister had managed the media, laying down an embargo for a couple of weeks until Duarte was ready for the attention. He had walked out of their first press conference less than an hour ago, knowing he hadn't been ready, but there was nothing to be done now.

The press had called him a walking ghost, a man returned from the dead. They had jumped at the chance to paint him as some kind of hero to fit their own sensational narratives.

No one seemed to understand that his survival was not something he wished to be celebrated for. Not when he was sure that his disappearance and the suffering he had endured had been entirely his own fault.

By rights, he *should* be dead.

He sat heavily against the back seat of the car, running his hand along the length of the long scar that traced the side of his head above his ear. It turned out that the nightmarish recovery process he'd endured after a gunshot wound to the head had been child's play compared with trying to fit back into a world where Duarte Avelar had ceased to exist.

As they drove away he watched the sun shine over the picturesque countryside hamlet that his family had adopted as their home after moving from Brazil. As a young boy he had been angry and homesick, barely even ten years old, but this quiet place had soon become home. Even when he had made his fortune, owning homes in every corner of the world, nothing had compared to the feeling of this small slice of peace and paradise.

Now…nowhere felt like home.

Everything was wrong. *He* was wrong.

He saw it in the glances his sister shared with Valerio, his business partner and best friend. They had witnessed his shifting moods, his restless lack of focus and his irritation with the debilitating headaches that could hit at any moment.

Two weeks previously, when they had been informed that he had miraculously survived, they'd both rushed to where he'd been kept, at an elite private medical facility on a tiny island off the coast of Brazil. Up until that point he'd had no memory of who he was, and had been singularly focused on rebuilding the physical strength he had lost during the months he'd spent confined to a hospital bed.

Talking to them had been painful, but he had started to recover some memories with their help. Coming back to England had been Dani's idea, and he had seen her eyes fill with hope that he would somehow come back to their childhood home and magically be restored to his former self.

It had worked to a certain extent. With their help, the gaps in his memory had begun to fill, but he still felt a strange disconnection from it all. Dani was determined to think positively, but Duarte felt nothing but apathy for the strange world he had re-entered. At times he even longed for the peaceful solitude of his anonymous life on the island, then felt guilt for his own selfishness.

In his absence, so much had changed. With every passing day he continued to be reminded of how people had moved on and adapted, growing over the hole he had left behind. Growing together mostly. He scowled, thinking of the look on his best friend's face when he'd revealed that in Duarte's absence he and

Dani had fallen in love and were now engaged to be married.

His best friend and his twin sister were going to be man and wife. The fact that their relationship had begun as a measure to protect Dani from the corrupt forces who had been behind his kidnapping had only angered him further.

It wasn't that he didn't want them to be happy. But they'd buried him. Mourned him. And then they had moved on—all while he had been trapped alone in a living hell.

His anger was a constant presence and it shamed him. They had done nothing wrong. No one could have known he was still alive. In fact, his father's oldest friend in Brazil had ensured that no one knew until the time was right.

But Duarte hadn't told them that part of the story yet… He hadn't told anybody. Telling the truth behind the events that had led to him and Valerio being captured and tortured at the hands of Brazilian gangsters would mean admitting his own part in what had happened. Revealing the secrets he'd kept from them both. Secrets that now had gaping holes in them, thanks to his memory loss.

Dani had been subtle, but pointed in her

questions about when he might feel ready to get back to work. Velamar, their luxury yacht charter company, was just about to open new headquarters in the US and in the Caribbean. It was something that he and Valerio had been building towards for more than a decade. His answers to her repeated questioning had been hostile and he had refused to commit to attending.

After the press conference that morning he'd told them both that he was going back to Rio for a while, to assist with securing one of the Avelar Foundation's charity developments— a sizeable portfolio of prime urban development sites in Rio De Janeiro, which had been the catalyst for all the trouble he had brought into their lives.

Of course the charity was only one of the reasons he was returning to Rio, but he hadn't told them that.

Dani had been stone-faced and had walked away from him without a single word. Valerio had been torn between them both, his mouth a grim line as he'd urged Duarte to take a large security detail and be careful.

He knew his sister was hurt by his distant

moods, but he felt stifled by her company, by her obvious happiness with Valerio and by her questions about his time in recovery. But he didn't want to talk—didn't want to remember the pain of learning to walk again and pushing his broken body to its limits. Not when he was so consumed with bringing down the wealthy criminals behind his ordeal and making sure they paid for their crimes.

The insistent chime of his phone grabbed his attention. The screen showed a text message from an undisclosed number.

We found her.

Duarte felt his body freeze for a moment before he tapped a few buttons on the phone to open an encrypted server. His team of private investigators and ex-law-enforcement operatives had been hard at work in the past week, since he'd set the course for his revenge. They'd already recovered and collated every photograph and video of him from the past year, trying to create a map of his movements. Judging by the most recent files added, they'd uncovered a wealth of photographs taken at a political event he had attended directly before his kidnapping.

He scanned through the countless images, one after the other, seeing that a trio of pictures at the end had been flagged for his attention. The photographs showed him standing away from the main podium area, towards the back of the large event hall. Something thrummed to life in his gut as he clicked through the files until finally a glimpse of long red hair made him freeze.

It *was* her. *Cristo*, he'd finally found her.

Of all his tortured dreams as he'd recovered on the island, those of the beautiful redhead had plagued him the most. When he'd first come out of a medically induced coma, the only clear memory he'd had was of her holding him as he bled out. He hadn't been sure if it was his imagination that had conjured such a vivid picture or if it was truly a memory he'd managed to retain.

She'd kept him warm with her body around his, her hand holding his own as she'd spoken his name so softly. Her bright silver eyes had been filled with tears, and the scent of lavender had cocooned him as she'd tried to stem the blood-flow.

'Duarte...please don't die,' she'd sobbed, before cursing in colourful Portuguese.

Her words had been like a mantra in his mind. *'You need to stay alive for both of us.'*

That voice in his mind had kept him going throughout his intense recovery process. And now he couldn't shake off the feeling that she was...*important*, somehow. That she was real. But, despite all the people that Angelus Fiero had tracked down and arrested in the last two months, there had been no mention of a woman anywhere near that shipping yard.

But now, looking at the photo on his phone screen...

One look at her face and he knew it was her. He knew she was real, not a dream. She had been his very own angel that night. She had saved his life with her bare hands, but she had left before anyone saw her.

Why?

He ignored the countless theories his mind produced, knowing none of them painted her as having nothing to hide. He would think about that later. For now, this woman was possibly the only link to what had happened that night and he needed to find her.

He looked up, noticing that they had arrived at a small private airfield outside London. His pilot, Martha, stood on the Tarmac to greet him, along with the small crew of one of the Velamar fleet of private jets.

Duarte smoothed a hand over his jaw as he tried not to think of his sister's words, begging him to forget his ordeal, to let the police continue to handle it while he focused on getting back to his normal life. Now, after seeing the woman's face, knowing she was real, he felt as if he was finally doing something that mattered. The cogs in his brain were turning, giving him purpose.

But was he just tracking her down to find out what she knew, or was it something more?

He brushed off the thought and dialled a number on his phone, hearing the rasping voice of his chief investigator as he answered the call and began griping about the various data protection laws standing in the way of facial recognition and searching for the mystery woman. Duarte growled back that he didn't care what he had to pay or what had to be done. He added that if his team had eyes on her by the time he landed in Rio their fees would be doubled.

The other man swiftly changed his tune.

'You will wait for my arrival before you make a move. Nobody is to approach her or bring her in—understand?' Duarte felt anticipation build within him as he growled the warning. 'She's mine.'

Nora Beckett took one last look at the empty space of her tiny apartment and felt the weight of uncertainty descend, choking the air from her throat.

She wouldn't cry. She'd done enough of that in the last six and a half months to last her a lifetime. Crying was for people who could afford that weakness, she thought miserably as she opened her phone one last time and looked at the list of missed calls and unopened voice-mails. The name on the screen read 'Papai'. Such an innocent word to cause such a violent reaction in her gut.

She placed the phone in one of the boxes, knowing she couldn't take it with her. As far as she was concerned she had no father. Not any more.

She'd thought she was almost free of his reach…

She'd thought she still had time…

Her powerful father had been in hiding somewhere outside of Brazil for months, and Nora had taken the time to finish her studies at university, cramming in as many repeat classes as she could to try to undo some of the damage of the last year.

She'd barely managed to scrape through her final exams when the first messages had begun to arrive. She had no idea if she would even be allowed to graduate with her patchy attendance record, but sadly, that was the least of her worries right now. She had to get out of Rio.

The open boxes on the floor overflowed with books on engineering and environmental studies. They were the only possessions she owned other than her small case of clothing, but they were too heavy to take with her. She'd already done far too much today, bending down and scrubbing the place all morning so she could get her meagre deposit back.

As though agreeing with the thought, her lower back throbbed painfully.

As she descended the five flights of stairs

to the street below she cradled the enormous swell of her stomach, taking care not to go too fast for fear she might jostle the precious cargo nestled within.

She had agonised over booking the four-hour flight to Manaus at this late stage of her pregnancy, but the nurse at the clinic had assured her that spending three days crammed in a bus to travel across the country would pose far more of a risk.

Her legs and feet had already been swelling painfully in recent days. And arranging her swift escape had put her under so much stress that her head throbbed constantly and insomnia plagued her. When she did manage to sleep she had fevered dreams of walking into her mother's arms in the quiet, peaceful safety of the remote animal sanctuary where she'd grown up on the banks of the Amazon.

She just hoped that Maureen Beckett would welcome her runaway daughter's sudden, unannounced return…and forgive her for the past five years of silence…

Whenever she thought of the last words they'd spoken to one another shame burned in her gut and stopped her from calling, but she had at least sent a letter. She'd written that she was sorry. That she'd been a naïve, sheltered eighteen-year-old with a desperate hunger to see the world and her father's promises ringing in her ears.

She'd received no response.

The sanctuary was the only place she could imagine raising her baby without fear or threat. She wouldn't be alone there, amidst the bustling community of ecologists and volunteers, with her fierce Irish mother at the helm. There was a small birthing clinic in the nearby village, and she'd arranged to rent a room with the last of her savings in the event that her mother turned her away.

But deep down she hoped her mam would forgive her.

It was the beginning of May, technically the start of the dry season, and yet the torrential downpour that now descended on Rio De Janeiro was like something from a catastrophe movie.

Nora tried her best to stay dry under the narrow porch, craning her neck to do a quick scan of the street. The bells from the cathedral nearby began to chime midday and, as she'd hoped, there was no sign of the dark blue car that had been parked in the alley all week. Even criminal henchmen took predictable breaks, it seemed.

Even though Lionel Cabo hadn't set foot in Rio in months, he still made it his mission to make his only daughter's life hell. Having her watched was only one of the ways he'd been tightening the noose, showing her the power he wielded. When she'd continued to ignore his calls he'd somehow managed to get to her landlord and have her evicted.

He knew she wouldn't dare go to the police, who were mostly in his pocket. He knew she was utterly alone here.

She bit her lower lip as she rubbed small circles on her aching lower back.

A small group of teenagers in hoods moved out from their spot in a nearby doorway as a sleek black sports car prowled slowly up the narrow street and came to a stop a short distance away. The young boys crowded around it, peering into the windows through the rain which was now beginning to ease.

Nora felt her senses shift into high alert. Usually the wealthy residents of Rio stayed far away from the more dangerous streets in this part of the city.

The teenagers moved aside as a tall figure emerged from the expensive vehicle. Rain instantly soaked his dark coat and he looked up, amber eyes glowing bright against the dark skin of a sinfully handsome face.

She was hallucinating.

Either her brain was playing tricks on her or she had fallen asleep, and was still upstairs, dreaming the same dream she'd had for more than six months.

The man closed the distance between them with a few long strides, stepping under the canopy with a strange stiffness to his movements. Nora fought to breathe as her headache intensified, her heartbeat thundering in her ears as she waited for him to speak.

'Nora Beckett?' he asked softly.

His voice contained the slightly clipped undertone of an English accent that she knew came from more than two decades living away from his homeland.

He extended a hand towards her in polite greeting. 'I hope you don't mind me coming to find you like this?'

Nora remained frozen, feeling as if she was watching herself from above, standing with this man who had Duarte's face and Duarte's voice. He dropped his hand after a moment, frowning, and looking back to where the boys were still investigating the exterior of his fancy car.

'I don't know if you remember me.' He spoke quickly. 'My name is Duarte Avelar. I was in an…an incident about six months ago—'

'Duarte Avelar is dead.'

Nora heard the hysteria in her own voice and willed herself to calm down, willed herself to find a logical solution for this madness.

'I'm quite alive, as you can see.'

His smile was forced, his movements strangely stilted as he reached for a split second to rub his hand across the slightly uneven hair growth on the left side of his head.

Nora followed the movement, noticing the thick dark brown line of puckered skin that began at his temple. What had once been soft, springy jet-black curls was now a tight crop that was barely more than skin at one side. She could clearly see the tiny marks where stitches had once sealed a wound that ended above his left ear.

The exact same place where she had tried to stem the blood flow with her own hands, had felt it spill over her dress and onto the cold ground around her feet.

She swallowed hard against the awful memories and focused on the man before her. His lips were still curved in a polite smile that was nothing like the man she had known. He seemed so real she almost felt as if she could reach out and touch him…

Frowning, she stepped forward and impulsively placed her hand on his chest. His sharp intake of breath took her by surprise, and she felt her insides quake with a strange mixture of fear and relief. She hardly dared to hope. She was unable to move, completely entranced by the blazing heat of his skin under her fingertips through the expensive material of his dove-grey shirt.

Almost of its own volition, her hand skimmed up a hard wall of muscle to where a glorious pulse thrummed at the base of his neck. *Alive.* She closed her eyes and felt a painful lump form in her throat at the cruelty of such a vision if this wasn't real. If it was just another one of her vivid dreams, after which she would awake in the middle of the night and expect to see him lying beside her.

Tears filled her eyes and she blinked them away, tipping her head up to find him staring down at her. His skin was still that rich caramel-brown, vibrant and healthy, so unlike the deathly pallor of that awful night.

She heard the tremor in her voice as she whispered, 'Duarte...this is impossible...'

'I've thought the same thing over the past months, believe me.' One side of his mouth twisted in the same sardonic way she remembered. 'But here I am.'

'You're actually here. You're alive...' Her voice was a breathless whisper as she felt a long-buried well of hopeless longing burst open within her.

Before she could stop herself, she closed the space between them and buried her face against his chest. He froze for a split second, and she feared he might push her away. She wouldn't blame him, considering she was essentially the reason he had received that scar in the first place.

She stiffened, bracing herself for rejection, only to feel his strong arms close around her.

She was instantly cocooned in his warm spicy scent and the glorious thumping rhythm of his heart. His beating, perfect heart.

Emotion clogged her throat as she was consumed by the urgent need to feel him, to hold on to him as though he were an oasis of hope in the unbearable desert of her grief. Her breathing became shallow and she was overcome with the need to kiss him, to feel his lips on hers once again.

From the moment she had first laid eyes on him in that crowded Samba club almost a year ago he had affected her this way. She had never reacted to another man with such primal desire, and he had told her that she affected him just the same way.

'You bring out the animal in me, querida.'

He'd whispered that in her ear right before their very first kiss. They'd almost made love on the beach, in full view of the pier. It had been madness, and she felt that same desire humming through her veins just from being in his arms now.

She leaned back, looking up and expecting to see a reflection of the intense emotion she felt.

Instead his face was utterly blank, and so confused it was like being doused with ice water.

This was wrong. Something was very, very wrong.

Suddenly she felt a tiny kick within her, wrenching her back to the present moment. She forced herself to take a step back, putting space between them as she composed herself and took in a lungful of air. The rain had died down and around them the sound of the boisterous youths filled the street.

Suddenly the weight of reality came crashing down upon her. If this wasn't a dream then it was a living nightmare. There was no question that this man was Duarte. And that meant her life had just become even more complicated.

She wrapped her bulky raincoat even tighter around herself and held her handbag in front of her stomach. If he was here, they were both in danger. This changed *everything*.

She looked around the streets once more, praying the blue car hadn't returned.

'How…?' she breathed. 'How are you alive?'

'It's a very long story.' He rubbed at his freshly shaven jawline. 'One that involves a medically induced coma and many months of painful rehabilitation. Let's just say I'm a hard man to kill.'

She heard the gasp that escaped her throat and closed her eyes against the image it created in her mind. He'd been alive all this time...in pain, broken...

She fought the urge to cling to him once again, never to let him go. But a tiny voice in her mind was screaming at her to run away as fast as she could and pretend she'd never seen him. Even if walking away from him now might be more painful than losing him the first time.

It was too much... She could hardly breathe...

'I hope you don't mind me tracking you down,' he said, and he spoke with a strange politeness to his tone that made her uneasy. 'You were there with me, the night I was shot.'

'Yes, I was there.' She frowned, watching the relief that crossed his face at her response. He smiled, and her heart seemed to pulse at the sight of it.

'Your care and kindness were the first things I remembered when I woke up.' His gaze softened for a moment before he seemed to shake himself mentally, then cleared his throat. 'I have a few things I'd like to ask you, if you wouldn't mind?'

'You don't remember me.' She spoke half to herself, processing the polite detachment in his gaze, the way he'd introduced himself to her—as though they were strangers.

It all came painfully into focus, like a movie replaying in her mind. He had no idea who she was…no idea what they'd been to one another.

'My injury has caused some slight memory loss. It's been a process—one I'm hoping you might help me with, actually.' He put his hands in his pockets and looked at her through his thick lashes. 'Is there somewhere private that we can talk?'

To any other woman his overtly calm posture would appear benign and almost welcoming. But Nora wasn't any other woman, and she knew when she was being baited. He might not have any memories of her, or their history, but that didn't mean he didn't still possess the killer instinct he was famous for.

He'd noticed her lengthy pause and the skin around his mouth had tightened with barely restrained irritation. She felt a shiver run down her spine. He wanted answers and he had managed to track her down. She suddenly felt as if he was a predator on the hunt and she a small rabbit heading straight for his trap.

She looked up the street and saw her bus, just beginning to turn the corner.

Duarte followed her gaze and narrowed his eyes.

'I'm sorry. I have to go. I have a flight to catch.' She forced the words from her lips, trying not to let him see the tears that threatened to spill from her eyes at any moment.

'Let me drive you to the airport. I just want to talk.'

Nora stared at the face of the man she had once loved. The man she'd *thought* she loved, she corrected herself.

If he said he had no memory of her, did that mean he had no recollection of what had passed between them all those months ago?

Guilt and anger joined the swirl of emotions warring within her. She had made her own mistakes, but he had ensured she was punished in return. He had shattered her trust and broken her foolish heart.

She had grieved for him and mourned the father her child would never have. But a small, terrible part of her had whispered that at least with his death she would be safe from his wrath. Her child would be safe.

She needed to get away. Fast.

If there was one thing she had inherited from her crime boss father, it was the sheer will to survive. She closed down her emotional reaction to his miraculous return and focused instead on the worst moments they'd spent together. The pain he'd put her through.

She lowered her hand to her stomach, reflexively protecting her unborn child from the threat of danger. That was what Duarte Avelar was to her, she reminded herself. Dangerous. That was what he had always been.

Nora opened her mouth to tell him she had no interest in answering his questions, but instead let out a silent gasp as her entire lower body spasmed with pain. Her handbag fell to the ground and she gripped her stomach, feeling the dull throbbing that had been torturing her back all morning shifting around to her front and burrowing deep inside.

The twisting heat took her breath away. She could do nothing but breathe for a long moment.

'Are you okay?'

His voice came from close beside her, and his hand was warm on her elbow. She pushed him away, not able to look up into his face. She needed to get on that bus before her father's men returned. She needed to get out of Rio today. But she couldn't think straight.

'*Cristo*, you're pregnant...' Duarte breathed reflexively, slipping into heavily accented English. 'You're really, really pregnant.'

'Excellent observation.' She spoke through clenched teeth.

'Do you need to get to a hospital?'

'No... I was just lifting some heavy boxes. I'm moving out of town today.'

She breathed in through her nose and out through her mouth, praying this was just the shock of him showing up on her doorstep and her body was simply reminding her to take it easy.

In the back of her mind she heard the noise of the bus drawing closer along the street. She needed to *move*. 'I'll be fine. I need to get to the airport or I'll miss my flight.'

She moved to walk around him, throwing her arm out to hail the *ônibus*, but then she felt another wave of pain tighten inside her abdomen so swiftly she cried out.

Clutching onto the nearest object for balance—a very firm male bicep—she squeezed hard and prayed that this wasn't the moment her child would choose to be born.

As that thought entered her mind she felt a strange pop and the trickle of what felt like water between her legs.

This could not be happening.

She kept her eyes closed tight, a low growl escaping her lips through the waves of pain that seemed to crash into her body.

'I think my waters have just broken.'

CHAPTER TWO

NORA WAS VAGUELY aware of the sound of a loud engine slowing to a stop beside them and the bus driver calling out to see if she needed help.

'*Não obrigado.*' Duarte's voice boomed with authority.

She wasn't sure how many minutes passed before she opened her eyes and saw the bus had gone. She looked down to find herself clutching him like a limpet and groaned inwardly. She knew she should feel embarrassed, but she was rapidly becoming unable to think straight—or stand up, for that matter.

'Is there someone I can call for you?' he asked. 'The baby's father?'

Fighting the urge to sob, she shook her head and closed her eyes as she began to realise the gravity of her situation.

He frowned, pressing his lips together in a firm line as he looked down at her small suitcase. 'Can you walk? I'm taking you to a hospital right now.'

She allowed him to hold her arm as they moved carefully towards his car. She'd just made it to the door when another pain hit. He seemed to understand that she was unable to move, and he took off his coat and draped it over her while she breathed and tried not to curse.

'It's too early…' she breathed. 'I'm not due for four and a half more weeks. I'm not meant to be here in this city.'

He helped her into the car, bending down to carefully buckle her seatbelt around her before he looked deeply into her eyes. Warm amber filled her up with the same magnetic strength she remembered so well.

'Just try to relax.'

'Are you saying that for my benefit or for yours?' she groaned, closing her eyes against the beautiful sight of him.

She heard him chuckle low in his throat and opened her eyes once more.

'I'm going to drive now, okay?'

She nodded, staring up at this man she had

once thought herself in love with, this man who now had no idea who she was.

This couldn't be happening. He couldn't be with her when she was about to give birth to her child.

Their child.

'I can't do this…' She closed her eyes once again, a sea of thoughts overwhelming her, and sent up a prayer to everyone and anyone who might be listening. To keep her safe. To keep her baby safe.

She felt a warm hand cover hers. When she opened her eyes he was looking at her, and there was nothing but kindness and concern in his warm whisky-coloured eyes.

Maybe it was the pain, or maybe she was just in shock, but she heard herself whisper, 'I've been so afraid of doing this alone…'

'You are not alone.' He squeezed her hand once more before turning and starting the engine of the powerful sports car with the push of a button. 'If my memory is correct, I'm pretty sure I owe you my life. I won't leave you.'

Duarte burst through the hospital doors carrying a wild-eyed pregnant woman in his arms.

The drive to the hospital had been blessedly swift, and free of the usual Rio traffic, but he had still feared they might not make it in time. He was famous for pushing himself beyond his limits, but delivering an infant in the passenger seat of a rented Bugatti was not exactly the way he'd imagined this meeting going.

This hospital wasn't the nearest medical facility, but when she told him she'd been attending a community birth centre in one of the poorest areas of the city he'd been hit by a strange protective urge so strong it had taken his breath away.

She was important to his investigation, he told himself. He needed her safe and well if he was to find out the information she might have.

Nora seemed to be delirious with pain as the nurses performed some preliminary checks. In between each contraction she became more frantic, her eyes glazed as she repeated that she had to get to the airport.

Duarte saw the questioning looks that passed between the nurses as they looked at the reading on the blood pressure monitor. The atmosphere in the room changed immediately. A bright red call button was pressed and soon the room seemed to fill with people—doctors and specialists, anaesthetists and paediatricians.

Nora clutched his hand tightly as the team moved around her, performing more checks. Her nails bit into his skin as she cursed through another intense wave of pain, her neck and back arching and her hair tumbling around her face in a wild cloud of red curls.

He felt utterly dumbstruck by her ferocious beauty. This woman was a stranger to him, and yet he was witnessing one of the most intimate moments of her life. He felt the strangest urge to reach out and comfort her, but was keenly aware of her boundaries. In the end he settled for the simple touch of his hand on top of hers.

Her back relaxed as the pain eased off again and she looked up at him, pinning him with eyes the colour of the sky after a heavy rain-storm at sea—deep silver with a ring of mid-night-blue. He was so captivated by her gaze that he hardly noticed as she looked down at his hand and frowned at the quartet of scarlet crescent moons left by her fingernails.

'Did I do that...?' she breathed, horrified.

Duarte leaned close to speak softly near her ear. 'Don't worry about me. This hand is yours for the duration. If you need to crush my fingers in the process, so be it.'

She shook her head, the ghost of a smile crossing her lips.

Duarte couldn't help it; he laughed at the crazy turn his day had taken.

She looked up at him through thick lashes, her eyes filled with surprise, and for a moment, Duarte felt the strong pull of *déjà vu*. His mind grasped at the feeling, but it was like trying to hold on to water and feeling its weight slip through his fingers.

Why did he feel as if seeing her was the key to unlocking some hidden compartment in his memory?

A young nurse chose that moment to interrupt, looking at Duarte as she explained that she needed to talk to the baby's father for a moment.

Nora's entire body froze, and a sudden lucidity that was almost akin to blind panic entered her eyes.

'No! He needs to leave.' Her voice lowered to a growl as another contraction hit her and her body began to arch forward. 'Get him *out* of this hospital.'

Duarte took a stunned step back just as another doctor entered the room and announced that they would be preparing her for immediate emergency surgery.

He was swiftly whisked away from her and taken down the hall to fill out some paperwork. The surgeon was a kind-faced young woman who assured him that his partner and the baby would be well taken care of.

Duarte opened his mouth to correct her, only to find she was already rushing away.

Keeping his mind occupied, he strode down to the nurses' station and set about filling in more paperwork. He had no idea what her date of birth was, or even her nationality so, against all his instincts, he opened her handbag and her suitcase and began to search.

For a woman who said she was leaving town, she had packed suspiciously light. Her bags contained no identification nor any clues as to where she might have been headed. She didn't even have a mobile phone. Baffled, he listed his own details as next of kin and made sure it was known that no expense should be spared in her care.

The nurse's eyes widened, her gaze flickering

between the name scrawled on the form and the long scar on the side of his face. For a moment Duarte was confused, but then he winced and cursed under his breath. In all the drama he'd forgotten that technically he was supposed to be dead. His family name was well known in this part of Brazil, thanks to their wealth of charity work.

He walked away from the stunned recognition in the woman's eyes, knowing that at some point he was going to have to contact Dani and explain how he'd come to be spotted in Rio, in hospital with a pregnant woman.

His shoulder twinged again, the pain hot and uncomfortable under his designer shirt. He had missed out on his evening swimming regime due to the long flight, and already he could feel his muscles seizing in protest. He seemed to be in a constant state of management, swimming against the tide and trying to live a normal life with his new damaged body.

After what felt like hours, he walked back down the corridor towards the operating theatre, feeling like a caged animal pacing its enclosure. Running a hand along the stubble growing on his jaw, he ignored the tension in his gut and instead puzzled over the way Nora Beckett had embraced him in the rain.

She'd thought him dead and had seemed overwhelmed at the sight of his return. She'd *known* him. He could have sworn he'd felt the echo of some fierce connection between them every time she'd looked at him. And yet she'd looked at him with fear in her eyes, and had bellowed for him to be taken from the room.

Something didn't make sense...

Unable to stay put a moment longer, he moved purposefully down the corridor to demand an update. At the same moment a nurse emerged from the double doors that led down to the operating theatres with a bundle of white linen in her arms.

'*Senhor*, I was just coming to get you.' She beamed. 'Baby boy is completely healthy. We'd like you to get settled in the suite while the team finish with Senhora Beckett.'

'Is she okay?' he asked, swallowing hard as he peered down at the small face, barely visible in the folds of material.

'The procedure required heavy anaesthesia and she is still sedated.'

The nurse ushered him down the hall to a

large private suite. The small bundle was placed in a cot beside the bed and then the nurse apologised as she was suddenly called from the room by a beeping device at her hip.

Alone, and utterly out of his depth, Duarte felt his chest tighten with anxiety as the infant began to wriggle. Did they usually abandon babies to the care of clueless billionaires around here? Give him a priceless antique catamaran and he would know how to take it apart and put it back together blindfold. But children had never exactly been a part of his wild playboy lifestyle.

Duarte walked to the side of the cot and peered down at the infant, its tiny features scrunched up, its hands flailing. Without thinking, he reached into the cot towards one tiny hand. His heart seemed to thump in his ears as his index finger was instantly grasped in a tight fist and the wriggling stopped.

'There you go, *pequeno*,' he murmured, rubbing his other hand against his sternum, trying to control the frantic beating of his heart as he marvelled at the force of the boy's grip. 'You can hold on tight if that helps. Your *mamãe* will be here soon.'

* * *

Nora opened her eyes to find she was still dreaming.

Often in the past six months she had fallen asleep to dream of Duarte, his amber eyes alive and full of happiness as he cradled their newborn baby. In that perfect life there was no anger or lies between them, no danger or threat of punishment from her villainous father.

She blinked at the vision before her in the luxurious hospital room—the painfully handsome man in his perfect designer shirt, shirtsleeves rolled up as he cradled the tiny infant in his powerful arms. She closed her eyes briefly at the memory of how she'd embraced him so passionately in her shock, then clung to him as he'd rushed her to the hospital.

But he didn't remember her at all.

A small tear slid from her eyelids and down her cheek as she realised that perhaps that was a blessing to them both.

To all three of them.

'You're awake,' that gravelly voice murmured from across the room. 'The nurse told me to tell you not to try to sit up by yourself.'

'My baby…' Nora croaked, her throat painfully dry. 'Give him to me.' She raised her voice, hearing the edge of panic creeping in but feeling too weak to hold it back.

Duarte frowned, but immediately did as she asked. The soft bundle was placed gently on her chest and Nora looked down at her son's perfect face for the first time.

'The nurse just fed him and she asked me to hold him for a moment.'

'Thank you...' Nora whispered, inwardly mourning the fact that her baby's first feed had not come from her.

She mentally shook herself, sending up a prayer of thanks that they were both safe. All those plans she had made for a natural birth had been thrown out of the window when the doctors had told her she was in an advanced stage of pre-eclampsia and they would need to sedate her immediately in order to operate.

Her headaches, the swelling... She was lucky they were both alive. She was lucky they had got to the hospital so quickly.

If she'd been alone...

Tears welled in her eyes at the thought.

'My sweet, sweet Liam,' she whispered, closing her eyes and brushing her lips against jet-black downy soft hair. He was beautiful, and so impossibly small she felt something shift within her. Something fierce and primal.

'Liam? An interesting name.' Duarte's voice seemed to float towards her from far away.

'It's short for the Irish for William,' she whispered, her eyes still fixed on examining the tiny bundle.

She almost couldn't believe that in the space of one day her life had changed so dramatically. She moved her fingertips over ten tiny fingers and toes, puffy cheeks and a tiny button nose. He was perfect.

She closed her eyes and placed her cheek against her son's small head as a wave of emotion tightened her throat once more.

'It's easier to pronounce than our version. My father always shortened his name to Gill.'

Nora refused to look up, unsure if he was baiting her somehow. But there was no way he could know she had chosen her son's name to honour the great Guilhermo Avelar.

She heard him take a step closer.

'You have Irish ancestry? You speak Portuguese like a native, but the red hair...'

Nora looked up and wondered if she imagined the shrewdness in his gaze, fearing that he was remembering… The reality of her situation came crashing down on her, dampening the euphoric pleasure of holding her child for the first time. She felt her chest tighten, but schooled her features not to show a thing, not wanting to give him any more information than needed.

'My mother is Irish, but I've lived here my whole life.'

'Here in Rio?' he asked.

'No. Not here.' She let her words sit and watched as he realised she wasn't going to play along.

He nodded once and took a few steps away, towards the window. Nora was briefly entranced by the sight of his handsome features in the glow of the afternoon sun. The blue sky formed a heavenly backdrop behind him, making him look like a fallen angel.

How could someone so beautiful cause her so much heartbreak? How could he remember nothing of the time they'd spent together? She'd told him of her Irish mother's lifelong work as an ecologist and about the remote Amazon village where she'd been born. He'd told her stories of his own idyllic childhood, and how happy they had been as a family until their move to England.

They'd bonded over a shared sense of having felt stifled and restless when growing up. She had never felt such a connection to another person, such an urge to speak the first thing that came into her mind. He had seemed like a good man then—before everything had become so twisted between them. But his anger had made him cold.

The last time they had spoken he had vowed to find her, to hunt her down and put her in prison alongside her criminal father. Even now she could clearly remember the simmering rage in his gaze as her father's men had dragged him away.

He might not remember that night, or all the events that had led to it, but he still felt that hunger for vengeance—she'd bet her life on it. Why else was he back here in Rio, digging around?

What would he do if he knew she had hard evidence that could put Lionel Cabo in prison for the rest of his life? The slim thumb drive sewn into the lining of her suitcase was the insurance she had used to secure her own freedom, but that same evidence would also serve as evidence of a damning connection. A connection that someone could use against her.

Trusting Duarte in the past had led to betrayal. Did she dare ask him for help, knowing that he might choose to use her past against her?

She closed her eyes and thought of the innocent life she had just brought into this battlefield. This should have been a moment of celebration for both of them.

For a split second she contemplated throwing caution to the wind and telling Duarte that Liam was his son. Maybe if she told him everything and explained herself he would see that she was not the same as her father after all. She had made her share of mistakes, but she was not the black-hearted criminal he had accused her of being.

But then she remembered his promise and imagined being thrown in jail for her crimes. She felt torn between silence and blind faith, but she was a mother now and she had a responsibility to raise her son. She couldn't risk it.

'I hope you don't mind me bringing you to

a different hospital.' He gestured around them at the clean sleek lines of the private mother-and-baby suite. 'I know the staff here from my charity work. It's one of the best facilities in the city.'

'I will try my best to repay you.' Her voice shook slightly and he instantly waved away her offer.

The gesture held so much lazy arrogance that her hands automatically tightened at the reminder that Duarte Avelar wasn't just rich, he was powerful. More powerful than any of the people she'd met while working for her father among Rio's high society.

Even without the fact that he was descended from one of Brazil's oldest dynasties, he was rich as Croesus in his own right. He was the kind of man who didn't have to worry about anything. He probably had world-class lawyers on retainer just in case he needed matters dealt with. If his memory came back, if he remembered what she had been a part of...

'Nora...' Duarte didn't move, but his eyes held her captive with their sincerity. 'Was there a reason you were leaving the city today, alone and in such a vulnerable condition?'

'That's hardly your concern.'

She kept her tone firm, the anxiety roaring within her a reminder of her own vulnerability. She *was* alone and he knew it. That meant it was even more important for her to keep the upper hand. Keep what little power she had left.

She looked up at his dark features, feeling the weight of fear crush any of the remaining traces of hope she might have had upon seeing him alive. She had far too much knowledge of what happened to a woman when she put herself in the orbit of a powerful man's control. Her son deserved to be safe, and she would die before she allowed him to be used the same way she had been as a child.

Her eyes darted to the window. She was trying to pinpoint where they were in the city. Trying to plan a way out, just in case.

Powerful men did not often give up their children—even illegitimate ones. Her own mother had found that out the hard way. Sometimes a child served as the ultimate form of control.

'I had to search your bag for identification in order to fill out your chart.' His eyes met hers, searching. 'I noticed you were packing very light. You don't even have a mobile phone or your passport.'

'I must have forgotten them at home.'

The lie fell easily from her lips and she felt a pang of relief that he hadn't found the hidden pocket in the lining of her luggage that she'd used to hold her savings, the thumb drive and her emergency documents.

'I thought that...so I had my assistant go back to your apartment to retrieve them.'

Nora fought the urge to growl, feeling his eyes on her, watching her reaction. Apparently his injury hadn't addled the entirety of his wonderful mind; he was still sharp. He must have been told that her apartment was empty, that she'd been evicted suddenly and without notice.

'What exactly are you asking me?' She assumed her best poker face, feeling as though she was walking a tightrope and might fall into the web of her own lies at any moment.

'Your landlord seemed terrified that he might be harmed and refused to give the reason for your eviction. In fact, he seemed quite concerned for your wellbeing, despite having no knowledge of your pregnancy. According to him, before today you had barely left your apartment in months.'

Nora felt her pulse hammer against her chest. How could she tell him that hiding behind the walls of her shabby apartment and living in anonymous squalor for months on end had been preferable to anyone in her father's criminal network seeing her growing stomach and using it against her? Her father would have known instantly whose child she carried, and he would not have hesitated to use the knowledge for his own gains. He'd always got her under his control so easily—it was one of his talents.

She had been eighteen when she'd first moved to Rio, home-schooled and painfully naïve, with her father's wonderful promises ringing in her ears. She hadn't reacted when he'd told her she stood out in all the wrong ways, with her simple outdoorsy style and her wild red curls. When he'd hired stylists to dress her and soften her looks she had foolishly seen it as him taking care of her. To a girl who had grown up fatherless and isolated, any attention from him had seemed wonderful.

Then he'd started asking her to gather small pieces of information for him. Her successes had been met with affection and gifts, and she'd never felt so happy and loved. She hadn't known then, but he'd been grooming her for his organisation, teaching her the tricks she would need to become one of his network of spies.

She'd obeyed his every command and completed every mission perfectly...until Duarte.

She looked up at the object of her thoughts and wondered which of the men in her life had hurt her more...

'I get the feeling that we knew one another, Nora. Maybe we were friends?' Duarte's whisky-coloured eyes bored into hers, assessing her with a razor-sharpness. 'If you're in trouble, I might be able to help.'

'I'm not in trouble.' Shaken, she tried to keep control of the conversation, hoping he wouldn't notice the tremor in her hands. 'And you are *not* my friend.'

'Well, that makes your earlier reaction to my reappearance even more interesting.'

Something within her bristled at the superior tone in his voice and the evident suspicion in his gaze. The Duarte Avelar she had so briefly known had not had this hardness in him. But, then again, that version of him hadn't been almost murdered as part of a blackmail plot involving the woman he claimed to have loved.

Still, she was a vulnerable woman with a newborn baby in a hospital bed and, as far as he knew they were perfect strangers.

Duarte stood up straight, his eyes sweeping over her and the small infant, something strange in his gaze. 'You've been through a lot today. I still need to speak with you, but my questions will keep until you have recovered.'

'Did you come back to Rio looking for answers…or for revenge?' She asked the question, holding her breath as she waited for the answer that would determine their fate.

His brows knitted together, and when he spoke his voice held a mixture of surprise and keen interest, as though he were dissecting a puzzle. 'You fear revenge from me, Nora?'

'You haven't answered my question.'

She spoke with steel, despite the frantic thrumming of her heartbeat. She was exhausted, and likely still in shock from the events of the past few hours, but she knew she needed to have this conversation for her son's sake. For her own sake too.

She forced herself to hold his gaze, trying not

to be entranced by the features that seemed like a mirror image of the tiny face on her chest.

He seemed to hesitate for a moment, his eyes shifting to take a sweeping look out over the city. When his eyes at last met hers, there was a haunted darkness to them.

'I came here to find out what truly happened in that shipping yard. For now, that is enough to satisfy me.'

For now.

Nora felt the threat of those words as clear as day. He might not know it yet, but he was on a direct path to retribution. His memories might be missing but his heart was still the same. He would never let this go. He would never forgive her for the part she'd played, unwittingly or not.

The silence stretched between them like an icy lake and she felt whatever slim hope she'd clung to begin to fade to nothing.

She looked up to see him watching her, his brow furrowed with concentration. Time seemed to stop as he opened his mouth to speak, then closed it, taking a few steps towards the window. He braced his hands on the sill, one deep inhalation emphasising the impressive width of his shoulders.

He was leaner than he had been before, his muscular frame less bulky but somehow more defined. The long, angry scar stood out like a kind of tribal marking along the side of his skull. She breathed in the sight of him, knowing that it might be the last time she could. That it *needed* to be the last time.

'I will leave you to rest for a few days.' He spoke with quiet authority. 'I am not so cruel as to interrogate you in your condition. But I *will* have my answers, Nora.'

She opened her mouth to order him to leave, fury rising within her at the barely concealed threat in his words, but she froze as she saw the unmistakable look of curiosity he sent towards the tiny baby she held in her arms.

'Seeing as you don't have a phone, would you like me to notify anyone about the birth?' Duarte asked, taking a step closer and peering into Liam's small sleeping face. 'Who is his father?'

CHAPTER THREE

NAUSEA TIGHTENED NORA'S already tender body, emotion clogging her throat as she inhaled and prepared herself for another performance. Another cruel twist, cementing her own web of lies beyond repair.

Just as she'd opened her mouth to respond, like an angel of mercy the nurse returned. Nora smiled politely as her son was lifted from her chest and put gently into his cot before the young woman began efficiently taking vitals, asking about her pain and making notes on a detailed chart.

Nora's vague realisation that she'd still been pregnant only hours ago was laughable, considering that her current sense of fear had completely overshadowed any of the strange sensations in her body from the Caesarean section.

She was painfully aware of his dark eyes watching her from the corner of the room. Her heartbeat skittered in her throat as the nurse widened her eyes at her blood pressure reading and then left the room, mumbling about getting a second opinion.

Nora fought the urge to call after the nurse and beg her to stay. *Please, stay.*

She wanted to delay the inevitable answer she had to give. The lies she needed to tell to keep her son safe. To keep them all safe.

In an ideal world she would celebrate finding out that the father of her child was alive and had returned to find her. In an ideal world this would be a reunion… But she had long ago learned that no happy endings lay in her future—only an endless fight for survival. The world she lived in was filled with nothing but danger and dire consequences if she took a single step wrong.

She had a tiny life relying on her now; it wasn't just her own future at stake. She could not let her heart lead her—not again.

'Who is the baby's father?' Duarte repeated.

She avoided his eyes as she folded and refolded the linen blanket on her lap. She bit her lip, trying to come up with a convincing lie, but found she simply couldn't. So she just went with omission instead, forcing words from her throat. 'I'm a single mother. I have no family here in Rio.'

Silence fell between them. She wondered if he was judging her for her situation, then brushed off the thought with disgust. She had far bigger problems in her life than worrying about the opinion of a powerful man who had never known the true cruelty of life at the bottom of the pecking order. He might think her in the habit of random flings, but that seemed preferable to the embarrassing truth.

The only man she'd ever let her guard down with was standing five feet away from her.

And he didn't remember a single thing.

She reached out and laid one hand on the small cot beside the bed, reminding herself of the tiny life that now relied on her strength. She needed to convince Duarte to leave, to forget all about her and Liam. Once that part was done, she would get back to her original plan.

Her heart seemed to twinge with the pain of knowing she would never see him again, but she forced the pain away, knowing she must survive losing him all over again for the sake of her son.

She had to.

'You said you wanted details about what happened that night? I'll write down everything I can remember and send it to you.' She spoke quickly. 'I'll tell you everything you need to know.'

Strong arms folded over an even more powerful chest as he stared down at her. Nora ignored the flare of regret screaming within her. The urge to confess everything and beg him to take her and Liam away from Rio, away from the reach of her father and the memories of all the mistakes she'd made, bubbled up inside her.

But she couldn't trust him—not after everything that had happened. She couldn't put her child's future in his hands, or gamble on the hope that he might be merciful. She needed to be strong, even if it meant doing something that felt fundamentally wrong to her on every level.

'Why do you act as though you are afraid of me?' Duarte asked darkly, his jaw tight enough to cut through steel. 'I pose no danger to you. You can trust me.'

'I trust no one—especially not men like you.' The words slipped from her mouth and she saw them land, anchoring him to the spot. '*Please…* just leave.'

She closed her eyes and lay back against the pillows, willing him away along with the one million worries that had come with his re-appearance in her life. She lost track of how long she lay there, eyes closed tight against the sight of him. She fought against the need to reach out and beg him to stay, to breathe in the scent of him one last time.

When she opened her eyes again he was gone.

She didn't cry, but the walls of the hospital room blurred into one wide canvas of beige and white as she stared upwards into nothingness.

If this was what shock felt like, she welcomed it—welcomed the cold that set into her fingers and the heavy exhaustion deep in her bones.

She had no idea how long she stared up at the ceiling before she drifted off to sleep, one hand still tightly clutching the railing of her son's cot at her bedside.

Duarte left the hospital in a foul mood, in-structing one of his guards to remain for sur-veillance. Whether that was to protect Nora Beckett or to ensure she didn't try to disappear he didn't quite know yet. But one thing was for sure: his mystery woman was deeply afraid of something. And, even though it made no sense, he had the strangest feeling that that *something* might be him.

The drive out of the city and high up into the hills to his modern villa passed in a blur. He had purchased the house a few years ago, but had very few memories of staying there. It was a visual masterpiece of clean lines and open living spaces, designed by an award-winning architect. Every feature took the natural surroundings into account, so that the building seemed to slot effortlessly into the rocky mountain face that surrounded it.

As a man who had taught himself to conceptualise and build ships just by observing the masters and trusting his feeling for what was right, he had a deep appreciation of design in all its forms. Usually the sight of this home filled him with awe and appreciation for such a feat of skilled, thoughtful engineering. But today he just saw a load of concrete and glass.

Duarte parked in the underground garage and found himself staring at the wall, processing the turn his day had taken in just a few short hours. He felt the sudden urge to grab a full bottle of strong *cachaça* and switch his mind off. To another man, the lure of getting riproaring drunk might have been attractive after a day like he'd had. But he was not another man, he reminded himself.

Perhaps he should have gone into the city, to one of the trendy upscale night spots along the coast. The bars would be teeming with beautiful women only too happy to help a man like him forget his troubles... But he doubted he'd even remember how to chat up a woman it had been so long.

Since he'd woken in the hospital all those months ago his days had been consumed only by recovery and, more recently, revenge. But maybe it was exactly what he needed. To indulge himself, to shake off the edge that had refused to pass since his dreams of the redhead began. Dreams of the woman who had saved him.

Nora.

He shook off the thought of her and made his way into the spacious entrance hall just as his phone began to ring. He looked at the name on the screen and answered the call from his father's oldest friend with a weary smile.

'Angelus—*tudo bem*?'

The old man was eager to hear about his meeting with the mystery redhead and apologised for believing Duarte had simply imagined the woman.

'She must have been the one to alert me that night,' Fiero mused, not needing to elaborate any further. They both knew what night he referred to. 'I got a text from your personal phone number simply stating the address of that shipping yard and the fact that you were in danger. You and Valerio had been missing for seven days at that point.'

Duarte swallowed his frustration at his lack of memories of his captivity. He had no clue as to what had occurred other than the scars that covered his body and the haunted look in Valerio's eyes. His best friend had refused to go into detail about whatever had befallen them during their long days and nights of captivity, stating that he was better off not knowing.

Nora had saved him—but why had she disappeared?

The thought suddenly occurred to him that

perhaps they had been together. Perhaps she had been taken captive too? But surely Valerio would have mentioned a woman.

Angelus interrupted his musings, launching into a detailed briefing on the latest developments in their joint sting operation.

The corrupt politician who had paid for the kidnap had already been brought to justice, shot by Angelus himself in self-defence. But they had evidence to prove the man hadn't been working alone. That there was a criminal kingpin behind the operation and he was hell-bent on taking control of the large area of land that the Avelar family owned and used for their charitable operations in Rio and Sao Paolo. Tens of thousands of tenants stood to be displaced and abandoned.

Thankfully, Angelus had arranged for the land to become untouchable, locked it into use by the Avelar Foundation, securing the homes and livelihoods of the families they assisted.

Duarte hadn't yet told Angelus that he remembered having lunch with that same politician just over a year before his kidnapping. Considering that Angelus was currently still recovering from near death because of his efforts to help Duarte, he didn't think his revelation would be well received.

It plagued him—why would he choose to meet with a man who so vehemently opposed the Avelar family's work in Rio? Their refusal to sell or redevelop prime land in what was considered an upper class area of the city had been the cause of a decades-long argument, dating back to his father's inception of the foundation. His parents had taken on the cause of the most vulnerable in society by building quality, sustainable housing projects. They had directly opposed and ignored the handful of corrupt developers that wanted to earmark the area for a luxury tourism development.

Duarte vaguely remembered the months before his kidnapping. He had been tired from spreading himself too thinly between Velamar and his own fledgling nautical design firm, Nettuno. When the Avelar Foundation had needed his immediate presence in Rio due to a large and embarrassing fire safety scandal, he'd been furious and resentful.

He'd had a few drinks with the politician and somehow they'd got into talks about what might happen if he sold the land with their family name kept solely as a front. He'd had plenty of his own charitable projects going on. He simply hadn't had the time required to pursue such a demanding cause.

Shame burned in his gut at the memory of that conversation.

But he would never have acted on it...he was almost sure. He vaguely remembered flying out of Rio determined to find another way to carry on his parents' legacy and uphold his duty to the people relying on the foundation.

His memories were non-existent from that point, but his passport showed that he'd returned to Rio three times after that trip. Whatever he'd come back for, he'd kept secret and eventually he was going to be forced to admit his suspicions to Angelus... That the person who had started this hell was possibly himself.

The infinity pool on the boundary of the villa had been serviced and readied for his arrival, as per his instructions. He had never been more grateful as he tore off his clothes and dived under the water in his boxer shorts. The fresh salt water engulfed him, cutting off the frantic hum of his mind and replacing it with a calming nothingness that soothed the anxious roar within him. Even if the relief was only temporary.

Anger and frustration had him doing more laps than usual, pushing his body to its physical limits as though reminding himself of his strength.

Teaching his damaged body how to walk and move again had been a nightmare, but he had done it. He had shocked his team of physiotherapists and smashed all their expectations. So much so that soon the staff and other patients would gather to watch him slice through the water at incredible speeds.

He'd thought that was the reason he'd become a minor celebrity in the small community, never realising that many of the staff had already been aware of his identity and had been paid heavily by Angelus for their silence.

Even without his memories he had felt the same connection to water, the same need that he'd had his whole life to swim or be out on the open sea.

It had been on that same beach that a strange man and woman had arrived and introduced themselves as his sister and his best friend. He'd remained silent as they tried to gauge how little he remembered. He soon found out that not only had he been a competitive swimmer and sailor throughout his teenage years and into his twenties, but he had apparently turned that passion into a career and was the co-founder of one of the biggest luxury yacht charter firms in the world.

Going from being an abandoned John Doe with no knowledge of his past to having his dream life presented to him should have been enough, he thought darkly. And yet he had been plagued by the thought that there was something vital he was missing—something he needed to do before his spirit would rest and accept his survival for what it was.

A second chance.

He lifted himself from the water with only minimal pain and stepped under the blistering hot spray of the outdoor waterfall shower. The heat loosened his muscles the rest of the way, ensuring that he would sleep without medication.

The heavy painkillers he'd been given on the island had become a dangerous crutch in the weeks after he'd awoken. His pain had been a relentless presence, along with the anxiety that stopped him sleeping or eating. Soon he'd begun to crave the oblivion those pills offered, and he had progressed to hoarding his dosages to achieve the maximum effect. Luckily, the nurses had recognised the signs and had made it impossible for him to continue down that path.

When a man was in constant pain, anything could become a vice, so he had adopted a strict, clean lifestyle and focused on healing his body naturally. But even now that he had his physical regimen under control, he still felt that restless hunger within him at times. It was as if he had come back to life with a great big chunk of himself missing, and no matter what he did... nothing filled the space.

His thoughts wandered back to the first moment he'd laid eyes on the woman from his dreams. Nora. How she had looked at him in that rain-soaked street, the shock and relief on her delicate features right before she'd embraced him. He'd felt something shift within him, as if something in his broken mind had awoken and growled *mine*.

Perhaps they had been lovers before his accident? She was certainly eye-catching, with her vibrant red waves of hair and large silver eyes. The thought of the two of them together filled him with a rush of sensual heat—until he remembered that she had been heavily pregnant with another man's child when he'd found her.

If they had been lovers, she had clearly moved on quickly.

Shrugging off the dark turn his thoughts had taken, he reminded himself of the more pressing matter that she was clearly in need of help and fearful of some unknown force. Afraid enough to pack up her life and move cities in an advanced stage of pregnancy.

He winced, remembering how he had told her he *would* get his answers. Suddenly the idea of getting answers seemed overshadowed by the idea that she might fear *him*. She was made of steel, that much was clear, and yet he'd seen flashes of vulnerability on her face that had made him tense with the primal need to protect.

His fists clenched tight and he shut off the water with an impatient growl. From the villa's hilltop vantage point he could see the last rays of the late evening sun glittering on the waves of the Atlantic below. He took a deep breath and wrapped a towel low on his hips, inhaling and exhaling the salty spray until he felt a sense of calm logic return.

If he had any chance of getting information from Nora he would first need to gain her trust. She was a new mother, in dire need of help, but he got the feeling that she would not accept help from him easily. Luckily for him, patience had always been something he had in abundance.

He let out a deep exhalation, a plan already taking shape in his mind.

He would get what he needed from Nora Beckett—one way or another.

'This can't be legal.' Nora stood by the edge of her hospital bed, her suitcase packed at her feet and the small bundle of her son in his baby carrier. 'It's been a full week and you've said yourself I am well enough to leave.'

'You're well enough to go home—not to fly across the country.' The doctor spoke in a firm tone. 'Miss Beckett. You will not be cleared to fly in your condition. I won't allow it. Recovery from pre-eclampsia needs to be closely monitored, and you will both need regular checkups here in Rio for at least another five weeks.'

'I can't stay here,' she said weakly. 'I have nowhere to go.'

'You have a home address listed, right here in Rio.'

Nora looked down at the form on the doctor's clipboard, seeing Duarte's name at the top and noting that the address listed was for his pala-tial villa up in the hills. A place where she had stayed before, numerous times.

'That's *not* my home.'

'We have been advised to stop you leaving.'

'Advised by who?' She raised her voice, look-ing around at the burly security man who had suddenly appeared outside her door and the slightly uncomfortable look in the doctor's eyes. 'Has someone asked you to keep me here?'

'I asked them.'

Duarte Avelar appeared in the doorway, im-peccably dressed in a sleek navy suit and light blue shirt. How unlucky could she get? He had become even more gorgeous, while she had been in a haze of sleepless nights with a newborn and had barely mustered the energy to brush her hair in the week since she'd last seen him.

'I told you I didn't need your help.' Nora squared her shoulders.

He gestured to the doctors and the guard to leave, closing the door behind them. His eyes drifted down, narrowing as he took in the small suitcase at her feet and the baby bundled up in the infant carrier she'd asked one of the nurses to order for her. Thankfully she'd set aside a small provision of cash for clothing and supplies for her son, but she hadn't expected to need everything so soon.

'You have no right to intrude on my privacy this way.' She shook her head in disbelief. 'I told you I didn't need your help.'

'I'm listed as your next of kin. The doctors called and filled me in on your plans to leave because they have concerns. I'll admit that I do too.'

His eyes met hers with an intensity that took her breath away.

'Packing a bag and then asking for internet access to book a flight?'

Nora swallowed hard, looking away from him and crossing her arms, ignoring the tender pain that still lingered in her chest from repeated failed attempts to nurse her son. She felt raw inside and out, and having Duarte reappear was just another thing sending her closer to the edge of her control.

'I am not doing anything wrong.' She forced a tight smile and deliberately slowed and calmed her voice. 'The doctor has said herself that both Liam and I are ready to be discharged. Not being allowed to fly has put a snag in my plans, but I will find a way.'

His frown deepened even more. 'Planning to leave the city?'

She looked down at her hands, feeling the heavy weight of her situation take hold. Without a flight, Manaus was almost three days away—at the other end of the country by the mouth of the Amazon. It was utterly ridiculous even to try to plan that kind of journey with a newborn and in her condition, putting them both at the mercy of public transport and cheap motels. She'd spent almost every last *real* she had paying to rebook her flight.

'I need to get out of Rio.'

She heard the desperation in her voice but didn't care. For all she knew, her father's men were waiting outside at this very moment. She had never felt so helpless and she hated it.

'Tell me why,' he said softly. 'Are you in danger?'

She bit her lower lip, looking away from him as she felt her eyes fill with panicked tears. She was losing every ounce of control she'd gained for herself, for her son. It infuriated her, feeling so utterly powerless.

Beside her, Duarte cursed softly under his breath and looked away for a moment. 'Nora, you must know you can't travel right now. If you need protection…' He seemed to measure his words for a moment. 'We've got about three minutes before the doctor returns, most likely in the company of someone from social services, who is going to ask some pertinent questions about the welfare of your child.'

Nora clutched at her throat, feeling it clamp tight with fear and realisation. She couldn't afford for anyone to go digging into her background right now. She needed to keep herself and her son out of her father's reach.

Closing her eyes, she inhaled deeply, completely aghast at the severity of her situation. Was this how she was starting her journey as a mother? Every single plan she'd made had gone wrong and now she was going to be investigated for child endangerment barely a week into her son's life!

'My home is nearby.' His eyes were steady on hers. 'You can stay there as my guest until they say you can fly. You'd have almost an entire wing of the house to yourself, along with anything you might need.'

'I can't fly for five weeks...' She half whispered the words.

'There is no time limit on my assistance,' he said softly. 'I believe that you played a vital role in saving my life and I would like to help.'

'Does this assistance come with a catch?'

She forced herself to look at him, to analyse his face so she could see if he was sincere. He seemed genuine as he spread his hands wide and shrugged one powerful shoulder.

'I believe you have valuable information that will help me to bring a very dangerous man to justice. I understand why that must seem overwhelming in your current position, so I won't press you for answers yet. Right now, it's my job to prove to you that I am trustworthy, and I am willing to wait and work for your trust.'

Nora bit her lower lip, focusing on calming her thoughts and laying out all her options in her mind. The way things stood, she was trapped between two utterly terrible outcomes. If she tried to leave alone she risked the attention of the authorities, and thus her father, who had webs in every area of the city. But the alternative was accepting an offer from a man who at any moment might remember who she was and what had happened and bring her whole world crashing down. A man she had spent six months mourning and dreaming of.

Could she hold herself together for five weeks?

'I want my flight changed to a later date, when I'm cleared to travel,' she said quietly, standing up straight in an effort to project an air of confidence. As though any of this was actually *her* choice...

'I will have it taken care of immediately.'

The door of the room opened suddenly and the doctor appeared, introducing a stern-faced woman in a pale grey suit as a representative from social services.

As Nora felt her body go slack, Duarte's hand reached out to her elbow and held her upright. She looked up at him, seeing the question in his eyes. Like a woman about to sign her own death sentence, she nodded once. She watched his pupils dilate, the briefest flash of triumph glowing in his amber eyes before he turned away, using his body as a shield between her and the others.

Nora felt as though she had entered a twilight zone version of her life as Duarte easily commanded the situation in a way that somehow managed to be both dazzlingly charming and authoritative.

As she watched his bodyguard gather her things, she tried to shake off the feeling that, after spending months ensuring she escaped her father's control, she had just volunteered to step into another shiny cage.

CHAPTER FOUR

DUARTE TRIED TO ignore his strange feeling of relief at having Nora agree to come under his protection.

Once they were safely within the gates of his home he allowed her some privacy to settle in, instructing his housekeeper to give her a tour of the rooms he'd had set up for her and to serve her lunch in private while she rested. He was painfully aware of the fact that he had no idea what a newborn needed, so he'd enlisted the help of his assistant at the Avelar Foundation, a young mother herself, and had instructed her to spare no expense.

Not wanting to crowd his guest, he spent the afternoon in various meetings at his city offices. With Angelus Fiero still recovering from his injury, it fell on Duarte to step in and oversee the final stages of locking down their lands for future renovation projects.

He returned to the house much later than he'd

expected, his back and shoulder aching from exertion. The house was strangely silent as he slipped into the kitchen and grabbed a pre-made salad from the refrigerator. Usually he took pleasure in cooking his own meals, but tonight he just wanted to eat quickly and get some sleep. He was not used to being back in the world of boardrooms and business deals, surrounded by the hum of conversation. It made him restless and edgy, as if he wanted to crawl out of his own skin.

He knew he needed to get back into practice if he had any hope of returning to his full workload as CEO of Velamar. His sister had sent him an email with details of the launch of their new headquarters in Florida the following month—a week of grand events in Fort Lauderdale to celebrate their new US and Caribbean charter routes.

A noise jolted him upright and he looked up to see Nora, standing frozen in the doorway of the kitchen. She held an empty baby's bottle in one hand and her small son in the other.

'Can I help?' he asked, standing up.

'No, thank you.'

She moved with impressive agility, balancing the infant in one arm as she prepared his milk with the other. Duarte frowned, making a mental note to call in a nurse tomorrow. If she wouldn't accept help from him, he'd ensure she got it elsewhere.

'I hope you have everything you need?' he said.

'You ordered a lot of things…' She met his eyes for a brief moment. 'I can't repay you for any of this.'

'I'm happy to help you any way I can.'

'In return for information?'

She spoke with a practised lightness to her tone, but he could see shrewd assessment in her gaze.

He placed both of his hands on the marble counter between them. 'I meant what I said at the hospital. Five weeks. I am a patient man, Nora. Right now my priority is keeping you safe while you rest and recover. Nothing more.'

She hovered in the doorway for a long moment, her red hair seeming to glow under the lamps of the corridor behind her. 'What if in five weeks… I still can't tell you anything?'

He heard the fear in her words, noting her use of the word *can't* rather than *won't*. He measured his words carefully. 'I think you should think about the kind of power I might hold over whatever it is that you fear. I might be able to help.'

She shook her head once, a sad smile on her lips. 'I wish it were that simple.'

She turned and disappeared back up the corridor, leaving Duarte alone with his thoughts.

Nora practically tiptoed around the palatial villa, in an effort not to run into Duarte. For the most part she was successful. She spent her days adjusting to Liam's needs, and was grateful for the help of the kind young nurse Duarte had provided to keep on top of her own aftercare.

Breastfeeding had turned out to be impossible with her terrible supply of milk, and she'd sobbed with guilt when her nurse recommended she stop before Liam had even reached his two-week milestone. Without the pressure of her own failure hanging over her, she found she became slightly more relaxed. In a matter of days, her blood pressure readings returned to normal range and she began to smile again.

She was slowly beginning to feel a little more

human, but still she found herself scanning the exterior grounds and refused to walk outside the house.

In the early hours of the morning that marked the start of her third week as Duarte's guest Nora awoke in a blind panic, her skin prickling with awareness as she jolted upwards in the gigantic four-poster bed. Blinking in the darkness, she placed a hand over her heart as though trying to calm her erratic breath. Her skin felt flushed, and the sheets were twisted around her legs as though she'd been thrashing in her sleep.

It wasn't the first time her dreams had been invaded in such a fashion, but this one had been by far the most X-rated. In it, Duarte had touched her with such gentle reverence, his eyes drinking her in as though she were the most beautiful thing he had ever seen. She had heard herself moan that she never wanted him to stop, her voice husky in a way she'd never heard before. She had felt every touch of his mouth as he kissed a path of sensual heat down her neck…

Shaking off the shiver of awareness that still coursed down her spine, she took a deep breath and peered over into the small cot beside her bed to ensure that Liam still slept peacefully. She adjusted his blanket and tried not to think of her handsome host or his frequent appearances in her subconscious.

If she'd expected Duarte to break his vow and demand answers, she'd been completely wrong. If anything, he'd gone out of his way to give her space. He spent much of the day out of the house, likely working somewhere in the city. Some nights he didn't return at all, like tonight.

She hated it that she was so hyper-aware of his movements, his presence. She'd tried her best to train herself to think of him as a benign stranger, but it was hopeless—especially while she was staying in this villa where memories of their time together assailed her.

Every time she walked into the living room she remembered the first night he'd taken her there…his mouth on hers as they failed even to make it to a bed. He'd been shocked to discover she was a virgin, and he'd insisted on bathing her afterwards. He'd sat behind her in a large claw-foot tub, overlooking the mountain view, and his hands had stroked over her body so reverently…

After that, she'd come to the villa countless times, always after the staff had been excused for the night. She'd been living in her own fantasy, imagining that she would build up to telling Duarte the truth of her identity and never incur his wrath or suspicion.

And all the while her father had been completely aware of her movements, plotting his revenge for her lies and deception. She'd been nothing but a pawn. A disposable entity to both powerful men in her life.

Now, lying back on the pillows in the silent house, she felt on edge. Earlier that day she'd tried to take a walk outside, for the first time since arriving. But while wandering around the courtyard, with Liam tucked tight against her chest, she'd thought she'd seen a familiar dark blue car parked at the end of the driveway. Her heart had stopped and she'd moved quickly back into the house, peering out of the window to see the car remain in place for another half-hour before slowly moving further down the road.

She'd had such a broken sleep tonight that it was possible she was being overly sensitive. It was only natural that she would be feeling the effects of her captivity. She wasn't technically a prisoner here, but she knew she couldn't leave. Not yet.

Frustrated, she gave up on trying to go back to sleep, wrapped herself in a thin cotton robe and clipped the portable baby monitor to the pocket. The clever gadget had been delivered the day after her arrival, along with a whole host of other items, including boxes and boxes of clothing for both her and Liam. In the haze of her sleep deprivation at the time she hadn't had the energy to insist she would pay for the items. But she knew she must repay Duarte somehow. She refused to fall under the spell of a rich man and then begin to feel like she owed him something.

Lost in thought, she almost missed the faint sound outside the house, but her heightened senses alerted her to the fact that something wasn't right. Frozen in place, she hardly breathed as the sound came closer to the large plate-glass windows that lined the back of the house. In the absence of the moon, she could see nothing but shadows and the crash of the waves in the distance below the cliffs made it hard to distinguish what exactly was out of place.

But then she heard it again. Footsteps on gravel, slow and deliberate. Heavy steps—much too heavy for the delicate, swanlike nurse or the housekeeper, neither of whom would be outside in the dark in the middle of the night.

Her brain made quick calculations as she moved instinctively to the side of the doors, out of sight. A tall shadow moved along the glass in her peripheral vision and Nora felt panic climb in her throat. All too quickly the quiet sound of the catch sliding sideways in the doorframe became apparent. To her horror, it seemed to have been left unlocked.

She watched as the door slid slowly open and the intruder pushed their tall, hulking frame inside.

Duarte felt his breath rushing in his lungs, hardly believing the events of this night. He'd been less than ten minutes from the villa when one of his security guards had informed him there was a break-in in progress. Two large men in a dark blue car had arrived shortly after midnight and managed to scale the gates.

Duarte and the guard had arrived just as the intruders had overpowered the second guard he'd left in charge of the surveillance of his home and its occupants.

Fury such as he had never known had possessed him as he had attacked the men and subdued them, using perhaps a little more force than necessary. His knuckles had become bloody, marking his white shirt and dark trousers, and he'd growled into his phone for his investigation team to send a van to pick the intruders up and take them for questioning. He'd left his security team to handle the rest, needing to get inside and ensure that Nora and the baby were unharmed.

Something about the two burly intruders snagged on his memory. He stepped into the darkened kitchen, feeling a memory surface like a television screen coming into focus. He froze with one hand still on the door handle, his mind conjuring an image of himself being thrown into a dark room, the smell of damp earth mingling with the scent of the sea in his nose. And then there had been Valerio's furious voice, asking him if the woman had been behind everything.

The woman?

He pulled at the details, hoping for more, cursing as he felt them slip away.

He heard the movement behind him too late. Something hit him with sharp force behind his knees, jolting his equilibrium and sending him down onto the porcelain tiles. He landed on his left shoulder. The pain lanced through him like fire, a primal roar ripping from his throat.

A blur of white moved in his peripheral vision—someone trying to step over him in the narrow space. On autopilot, after months of running on his survival instinct he reached out, grasping bare flesh. The skin was butter-soft, his brain registered, and his thoughts were confused between defence and attack. He tightened his grip but did not pull, straining his eyes upwards in the darkness.

His hesitation was all his opponent needed to turn the tables.

Within seconds he found himself pinned to the floor, with something cold and metal pressed tight against his sternum. A familiar lavender scent drifted to his nostrils and his eyes finally adjusted enough for him to make out a cloud of familiar red curls.

'Nora...' he breathed, shocked to feel his

body instantly react to the sight of the wide-open split of the white nightgown she wore. 'It's okay. I'm—'

'I've got a high-voltage electronic Taser here, so I wouldn't try to move.' She cut him off, pressing her knee down harder onto his shoulder to prove her point. 'I've already pressed the panic button, so don't try anything.'

'Listen, I'm not—'

'How did he find out I was here?' she gritted out, and there was a slight tremor in her voice even as she kept her aim firmly at the base of his throat.

Duarte froze, taking in the confidence in her pose, the steel in her voice. He had to admit he was both impressed by such obvious skill and worried about where she'd honed it. Why it might have been a necessity.

Suddenly, her hurry to leave the hospital took on a much darker tone...

'I don't know who *he* is.' He spoke slowly, trying not to wince at the pressure of her knee on his injured shoulder. 'I'm here because I own this house.'

She froze, easing up on her pressure with

a single jerky movement. Her voice was a shocked whisper. 'Duarte...?'

'In the flesh.'

She scrambled to her feet and Duarte tried but failed to avert his gaze from another tantalising glimpse of those long bare legs. The lights were turned on suddenly, momentarily blinding him as he pulled himself up to a seated position. His left arm hung limply at his side, and a familiar burning pain was travelling from his neck to the top of his shoulder blade before disappearing into numbness.

Partially dislocated, he'd bet. After months of gruelling physiotherapy sessions, he recognised the symptoms of his recurring injury.

'I'm so sorry... I thought you were someone else.' She stood on the opposite side of the kitchen, arms folded across her chest. 'A burglar.'

'Do you routinely confront dangerous intruders and pin them down for questioning?' he drawled, moving to stand up.

The pain in his shoulder intensified, taking his breath for a moment and putting stars in his vision. He sat back against the glass door with a growl.

'You're covered in blood!' She moved towards him, her face a mask of shock and concern. 'What on earth…?'

'Not from you.' He breathed deeply against the lancing pain. 'I was in a fight.'

His first instinct was to brush off her concerns—male pride winning out over his need for assistance. His shoulder was the last stubborn remnant of his injuries, along with the memory loss. There was an angry, bitter part of him that would rather languish in agony than admit any further weakness. But then Nora leaned down, gently placing one hand on his arm, and his mind seemed to go blank.

'But this is from me.' She spoke softly, the flash of her silver eyes briefly meeting his own. 'Is it your shoulder or your arm?'

'Shoulder. It wasn't entirely your fault.'

He felt the warmth of her skin through the material of his shirt as she lifted the sleeve. The scent of lavender grew stronger.

Duarte closed his eyes, clearing his throat. 'It's fine. It's an old injury.'

She snatched her hand back as though burned and he tried not to mourn the loss of contact.

With a deep inward breath, he pinned his

arm to his chest as he slowly moved to stand up. 'Besides, I was lucky you were far too busy threatening me and asking questions to do any real damage.'

The slim black device in her hand caught his eye; he could now see it was not a Taser at all but a digital monitor. The small screen showed an image of a sleeping infant. A hollow laugh escaped his lips.

Nora frowned, realising he'd noticed her deception. 'I… I had to think on my feet.'

'You're quite practised in that, it would seem.'

Her posture changed at his comment, her shoulders straightening and her lips pressing into a thin line. But still she offered no explanation for her belief that she had been found by someone. Nor did she explain who that someone was.

Duarte had always been good at reading people, and right now he could see distrust settle into her eyes. She was the very definition of a flight risk, and if he had any hope of keeping her safe and finding out what her connection to his kidnapping was he needed to keep her here.

Almost as though she could hear his mind

working, she took a step away, towards the living room. 'I should be getting back to bed...'

'Not so fast.'

She turned back and placed both hands defensively on her hips.

'I need your help with this,' he said. 'I don't think your nurse would be happy to be awoken at this hour.'

'I... I'm not a medical professional. Could you take something for the pain?'

'I know what I'm doing. I just need your hands.'

'My hands?' she repeated, eyeing the space between them with a strange expression.

Duarte tried not to feel affronted by her obvious reluctance to touch him. 'It's the least you can do, really, after you knocked me to the ground without effort.' He raised a brow in challenge.

When the barest smile touched her lips Duarte felt something inside him ease. She had clearly known fear in her life, and to think she had been afraid of him had made something dark and heavy settle right in the centre of his chest.

When she moved to stop beside him he deliberately avoided her gaze, needing a moment to clear his thoughts and ready himself for the manoeuvre.

'Will it hurt?' she asked quietly, her teeth worrying her lower lip.

'It's not without pain, but it's quick and then I'll be able to sleep. If you let me guide your hands, I'll show you.'

She placed both her hands into his much larger ones and Duarte felt again that strange echo of memory in the back of his mind as he took in the contrast of her porcelain skin against his dark brown tones. Brushing off the sensation, he placed her palms on the front of his shoulder, right where the pain burned most. As expected, her touch intensified the discomfort, but he instructed her to hold her grip. Her eyes were wide with fear and yet she did as she was told, keeping her hands steadfastly in position.

He told her how and when to apply counter-pressure and then did a quick countdown, biting down on his lower lip as he quickly guided his joint to where it needed to go with a swift jerk. The muffled roar that escaped his lips was quite mild in comparison to other times, when he'd been forced to do this alone.

He took a few deep breaths as the pain ebbed, and when he opened his eyes she was in front of him with a glass of water and two aspirin, which he accepted.

'That's not the first time you've done that...' Nora frowned at him, her expression troubled as she watched him drink the water, leaving the medication untouched.

'My memory is not the only part of my body that has been injured. I have a whole collection of scars owed to my time in captivity and the men behind it all. They were an energetic bunch of guys.'

Duarte thought of the memory he'd recovered earlier and felt a shiver run down his spine.

She stood close enough for him to see her eyes move to the long thin scar that moved from his temple down behind his ear. 'Duarte, I'm so sorry.'

He hadn't heard her speak his name since that first day in the rain. The sound of it on her lips, the way it rolled smoothly off her tongue... something about it called to him.

'Why should you be sorry? It's not your fault.'

At that she looked away, clearing the glass into the sink. With her back turned, Duarte took a moment to sweep his gaze along the length of her body, noticing her narrow waist and lush curves. It had only been a month since she'd given birth and the woman looked like she could step onto a catwalk.

His initial attraction to her had deeply perplexed him, considering her delicate condition, as had the depth to which she had become engrained in his thoughts in the weeks since. He'd deliberately been staying late at work in the city so he could get past whatever madness had taken over his mind since finding Miss Nora Beckett and becoming her unwitting protector.

He was not usually the kind of man who got off on rescuing damsels in distress; he didn't feel the need to bolster his own masculinity. She was a beautiful woman and his libido responded to her as such—nothing more. The fact that he had not felt a similar attraction to any other equally attractive woman was just circumstantial.

Although truthfully, he hadn't been looking at women very hard, preferring to dive deeply into his work and avoid distraction as he fought to make up for the time he'd lost.

He had promised her five weeks before he would question her again, but tonight had changed everything. The suspicions he'd had that she was in danger had just been confirmed with that break-in—as well as her words as she'd pinned him down—and he needed answers.

Nora took deep breaths to push down the wave of sorrow that threatened to overtake her at seeing the extent of the pain Duarte had suffered up close. She had felt the strange effects of her hormones shifting since Liam's birth, but this was so much more. This was an echo of grief. The tears fell fast and heavy down her cheeks as she tried in earnest to turn her face away from Duarte's perceptive gaze.

'Are you crying?'

She heard him move from his seat and his hand was suddenly on her shoulder, turning her to face him before she could wipe her face or move away. His feather-light touch gently guided her chin so she was forced to look up at him.

'You didn't hurt me, honestly.' He spoke quickly, one hand covering hers and gently stroking across her knuckles with the pad of his thumb.

She shivered, remembering him doing that before, what felt like a lifetime ago. She felt an insane urge to ask him if he remembered that night. If he remembered that he had told her how breathtaking she looked right before he'd kissed her senseless.

It had been their first kiss—the first of many over the long month of their whirlwind romance.

With his golden eyes on hers, Nora experienced a mad desire to lean in and feel his lips under hers again. Just one more time. She felt her tongue trace the edge of her own bottom lip, saw him follow the movement. His fingers flexed on her wrist and she could see a muscle in his jaw tick ever so subtly.

'Why can't I stop thinking about doing this?' he murmured, his eyes dark as he leaned forward slightly and brushed his lips across hers.

Nora inhaled sharply at the contact, hardly believing it. Judging by the sudden widening of his eyes, he was just as shocked at himself.

But the shock was short lived and Nora reached up on tiptoe and wound her arms around his neck, touching her lips to his again, seeking the heat of him.

Without warning, he took a step forward and spanned her waist with his big hands, holding her in place as she was pressed back against the kitchen units. The sleek wood was cool against her back and the hard, blazing heat of him engulfed her front. There was no softness in his kiss now...only fire and need. He somehow managed to be delicate even as his lips took hers in an almost brutal sensuous rhythm.

She heard herself moan against his mouth and felt him move even closer, one hand cupping her jaw as he deepened the kiss.

In the months after she'd lost him she'd lain in bed and tried to conjure up the memory of his kisses. They'd only spent a month together—a month of scattered secret moments in between his travelling and her own duties to her father's organisation. They'd spent most of their time in bed...and yet it had felt like so much more.

She'd thought her memory vivid, but right now she knew nothing had done justice to what it actually felt like to be in his arms, his sinful mouth demanding and coaxing... And she also knew exactly what it would feel like to guide him up to the master bedroom and re-enact every detail of her dreams...

She froze, pressing her hands against Duarte's chest and putting a few inches of space between their lips. He frowned, his amber eyes black with desire. And then that frown deepened and she felt the atmosphere suddenly shift.

Duarte took a few steps away, bracing his hands on the marble counter of the kitchen island as he continued to breathe heavily.

'You have been lying to me, Nora.'

Duarte's voice was a sharp boom in the stillness. He turned back to face her, amber eyes narrowed with suspicion.

'That was not the first time we've kissed, was it?'

CHAPTER FIVE

NORA CLOSED HER EYES, knowing she had made a fatal error.

'Answer me,' he demanded.

All trace of passion from their kiss had gone from his face.

'No. It wasn't the first time.' Nora whispered, closing her eyes tightly as if to block out the weight of her words as she spoke them.

'We were together.' He said quietly.

It took her a moment to process the fact that his words were a statement rather than a question.

A strange look transformed his dark features. 'We were…lovers.'

His words were like a whip against her frayed nerves and for a moment she feared that he had got his memories back—that he would figure out that he was Liam's father and she would be completely at the mercy of his anger. But then she looked up into his eyes and saw a brief flash of uncertainty as he waited for her to speak.

She had always been a terrible con-artist. Her father had tried and tried to toughen her up and mould her to fit in with the other female operatives in his criminal empire, Novos Lideres. She was too innocent, he'd said. But that innocence had long ago been taken from her in so many ways.

She straightened her shoulders and met Duarte's eyes. 'We went on a couple of dates, Duarte. I saw no reason to further complicate things for you over a minor detail.'

'You are still lying.'

His words were a menacing growl. He took a step forward, closing the gap between them.

'My mind may not remember you but my body does. I know that if I kiss a certain spot on your neck you will lose control and your legs will begin to shake.'

Nora gasped, shaking her head in an effort to stop him. 'You're mistaken.'

'Stop! No more lies between us.' His voice was a seductive whisper. 'I remember touching you, Nora. I remember your beautiful face as you climaxed with the most delicious whisper of a scream.'

He looked into her eyes and Nora was utterly helpless, unable to move under the sensual weight of his amber gaze.

'I suddenly know all of these things and yet everything else is still in shadow. How can that be?'

Nora wasn't sure whether he was asking her or himself, but she inhaled a deep shuddering breath and found that the few distraction tactics and acting skills she was able to draw upon had thoroughly escaped her. She felt a mixture of arousal and fear creep up her spine, holding her paralysed and powerless to do anything more than stare at him in damning silence.

'Am I still mistaken?'

Nora closed her eyes and felt the echo of their passionate whirlwind affair rush through her like a hurricane, destroying all the hopes she'd had of talking herself out of this.

'It was a casual thing. Barely more than a few weeks until it was over.' She forced the words out and watched as Duarte's eyes blazed with triumph, then narrowed on her once again.

'When?' The word was a harsh demand.

'A year ago. Five months before your kidnapping,' she said, wondering if he was mentally doing calculations.

The idea that he was suspicious enough to ask for that confirmation was more fuel heaped onto the fire of anxiety within her. She had told him the truth. Their short-lived fling had ended the day he'd walked out of her father's home. But of course there had been that crazy day when he had appeared in the rain outside her university a couple of months later...

An involuntary shiver went down her spine as she remembered the anger and frustration of their conversation erupting into a single desperate explosion of passionate kissing in his low-slung sports car. They'd been parked near the beach in broad daylight, and she had shocked herself when she had moved to spread herself over him and felt Duarte enter her unsheathed.

The madness had only taken them briefly, before they had realised what they were doing and stopped, but apparently that was all it had taken for her to fall pregnant.

She wouldn't regret it—not when it had given her the greatest gift of her life. Her son.

Duarte took a deep breath, opening his mouth

to speak, but just then they were interrupted by the arrival of one of his bodyguards in the doorway. Nora was shocked to see that the man was covered in blood and had a split lip. It suddenly dawned on her that Duarte had told her he'd been in a fight. What had happened?

'The intruders have been removed, sir.' The guard spoke quietly but his rasping voice carried on the wind. 'Senhor Fiero has confirmed that they are members of Novos Lideres.'

Nora felt the ground shift beneath her.

'There's been a break-in and you didn't tell me?' She gasped, feeling her body begin to shake as she desperately grasped for the baby monitor, half expecting to see her father's face there instead of her peaceful, sleeping child.

'Thank you—you can take the rest of the night off.' Duarte's mouth was a grim line.

'That's not all, boss.' The guard flashed a glance towards where Nora stood. 'I don't think they were here for you. There were months' worth of surveillance pictures and notes all over their car...photos of her.'

Duarte's face turned to pure thunder as he instructed the guard to gather the evidence and bring it to his office.

Once the man was gone, he advanced on Nora. He was dangerously still, his arms crossed as he looked down at her like an angry god. 'Have they approached you since that night in the shipping yard?'

'I knew I was being watched,' she answered truthfully.

He closed his eyes, torment in every inch of his face. 'This is why you fear me. Why you have been so mistrustful of my help. I'll bet even now you are making plans to run. To disappear from here.'

'Running is the only defence I have to keep my son safe. Away from the crossfire. From all of you.'

'All of us?' His brow darkened with sudden ferocity. 'You consider me the same as *them*?'

Nora turned to walk away, but her progress was hampered by a strong, muscular arm against the doorframe. She looked up to find him dangerously close, his eyes twin fires of fury.

'Don't *ever* compare me to that lowlife gangster and his cronies again.'

'You say you're trying to help me, but we both know why you've really taken me under your protection.' She steeled herself, determined not to back down in the face of his anger. 'You're keeping me here to get information against your enemies. What makes you any different?'

'I don't take people against their will.'

'Well, that's good news for me.' She felt her breath expand painfully in her chest. 'Because I won't be staying here a moment longer to be used as a pawn in your game.'

'I have been up-front with you from the start. I do not use women.' He moved forward, pressing his hand to her cheek and forcing her to look into his eyes. 'Whatever this connection is between us, it is not some kind of ploy. I didn't plan that kiss.'

Nora blushed, remembering the heat of his mouth on hers, but she pushed the feeling away. 'That is another reason I can't stay here.'

'You can,' he said softly. 'You can choose to be a witness in my case and help bring a criminal to justice. You can choose to trust me to protect you.'

She shook her head, hardly believing the words coming out of his mouth. He spoke of trust. What would he do if he knew the truth of her terrible past. Right now, he was assuming that she was an innocent victim, caught in the crossfire of his war. That she could simply go on the witness stand and give evidence without repercussions.

She closed her eyes, thinking of her father and his clever net of spies and his unending power. He would likely pay the judge to throw her in jail while he walked away with a smile on his face. She was simply circling under his net and he was waiting to make his move and catch her. She knew how he operated. She knew that even if he didn't know about Liam yet, the very thought of his daughter reunited with Duarte Avelar would be enough to tip him over the edge into one of his rages. He would want Duarte dead for sure this time. And he would make sure she watched it happen.

And her son? She shuddered to think of Lionel Cabo using Liam in his games.

Panic edged her voice and she didn't try to hide it. 'I can't be a witness for your case, Duarte. I can't willingly put myself in danger like that just so you can have your revenge. I have to protect my son. I just want to get away from all of this and raise my child in peace.'

'Nora, this isn't about me getting revenge

for myself.' He walked to the window, turning his back to her. 'Those people almost burnt down a tower block full of apartments with living occupants inside. *My* tower, that *I'd* refused to sell to them. They have no morals, no limits when it comes to getting what they want. Those apartments were filled with hundreds of the most vulnerable people in society: elderly couples, people with disabilities and single mothers with their children.'

'The fire safety scandal...' She froze, remembering him telling her the reason he'd been in Rio, trying to save his parents' housing foundation. 'That was Novos Lideres?'

Duarte nodded. 'There is proof of a politician's involvement. A politician who was in Lionel Cabo's pocket. A friend of mine pursued the evidence and was almost killed as a result. But that politician was our only hope of pinning the crime on Novos Lideres and now he's dead. Cabo thinks he's untouchable. One of the things my business partner Valerio told me about the beatings we endured was that they threatened to kill my sister. They have no respect for human life, Nora.'

His fists pulled tight as he spoke the words

and Nora was quiet for a long moment. Up until now her decisions had been solely focused on how to keep herself and her son as far away from this mess as possible. To keep them safe and out of her father's nefarious clutches. But in walking away would she actually give her father more power? She had evidence that could put him away; she was an eye witness to many of his crimes.

Wrapping her arms around herself, she shuddered out a long breath and stared at the ground. Perhaps if she helped Duarte he might forgive her. More importantly, she might undo some of her own poor choices and finally be able to forgive herself.

Until Duarte, she'd told herself that the effects of her father's business dealings had only been on the money and power of wealthy men. She had fooled herself into thinking that she wasn't a true criminal if she wasn't hurting people. The truth was, every time she'd stolen information before feeding it back to her father it had hurt someone in one way or another. There had been political coups, corporate espionage... But she had never considered that perhaps her father had only ever let her see areas of his business that wouldn't scare or upset her. She had been unbearably naïve not to realise that her actions had hurt vulnerable people through cause and effect.

Her silence was part of the problem.

When she looked back up Duarte was assessing her with his shrewd gaze. She shivered to think what might be going on in his mind. She was fast realising that keeping her son away from all this was impossible. Perhaps she'd be better off choosing the lesser of two evils and putting her faith in the man in front of her.

'I don't want to let them get away with it,' she said quietly. 'I don't want to be afraid any more.'

'Such a fierce little angel you are.' His eyes blazed with triumph.

'I'm far from an angel…'

She heard the hitch in her own voice and felt an urge to tell him everything. Every terrible detail of her sins. She craved his forgiveness. She craved the bond they had once shared— before the reality of her awful family connections had torn it all apart.

'I have a house a short helicopter ride down the coast. I'll help you pack now and we can have your nurse flown in for check-ups each day.'

'Now...?' she breathed, looking out at the inky blackness of the sky.

'It's best if we leave before dawn.' Duarte's voice was quiet and filled with sincerity. 'Let me keep you and your son safe.'

Our son. Something inside her shouted.

She felt a heaviness in her chest in the region of her heart. *Tell him*, it said. *Tell him everything.*

But she couldn't. Not until she was sure of him and of the man he now claimed to be.

An uncomfortable thought flickered in her mind. If he was truly a good man and she had kept his son from him...did that make her a villain all over again?

'I'm not ready to make any statements yet, Duarte...' She steeled her voice, trying to muster some strength. 'But I'll come with you because I can't stay here. I want to help you, but I need some time to think about all of this, to make sure my son and I will be safe.'

'I'm a patient man, *meu anjo*.'

They both froze at his use of the endearment. Nora's heartbeat seemed to thump in the region of her ears.

After a prolonged silence she mumbled that she would go and get packed before quickly turning away from the haunting amber gaze that saw far too much.

Duarte walked out onto the terrace and made a quick call to order a helicopter from one of his trusted private firms. Paranoia had his head snapping up at every small sound.

He sat down heavily in the nearest deckchair and rubbed a hand down his face, feeling the dull pain still throbbing in his shoulder. His skin seemed to be on fire after that surprising embrace and the revelations that had followed.

He closed his eyes, remembering the softness of Nora's hands on his skin.

They had been lovers.

The faint memory of their connection had come to him the moment her lips had first touched his. He'd seen her underneath him… over him… Everything else was still in the shadows, as though the way his body had responded to her wouldn't let him remember anything else.

The moment she'd admitted the truth he'd immediately thought of the child. But unless she'd had a year-long pregnancy, the dates didn't match. The boy had even been born early, he reminded himself. He should have been relieved, but something within him had been quietly furious at the thought of her finding pleasure with another faceless man and conceiving a child.

The image of her fiery passion being given to someone other than him made his fists clench painfully. He briefly considered asking his team to find out who the man was, simply so he could land a punch on the bastard's face for abandoning his pregnant lover...

Duarte might have spent most of his twenties enjoying women in all their forms and wonders, but he had always used protection. And if by chance one of his lovers had ever become pregnant he would have done his duty and cared for his own flesh and blood.

Nora was a mystery to him in so many ways still, but this new knowledge of their intimate history together had changed something within him. He no longer felt adrift and lost in his own body. That single kiss seemed to have created a tether between them, from his solar plexus to hers, reaching out across the house and pulling her towards him. He could feel her presence like a moth being drawn repeatedly to the warmth of a burning flame.

He knew it was a bad idea to want her. He knew there was a chance she would refuse to tell him the truth of how she'd ended up in the shipping yard with him. And yet still he imagined having those soft curves underneath him once more. He imagined hearing her cry out her pleasure in real time and seeing if the vague memory he had did it any justice.

He didn't know how long he sat, staring out at the blackness of the night sky, but by the time the distant sound of rotor blades sounded around him he had made his decision.

He would have her in his bed again.

As the helicopter began to descend over the small coastal town of Paraty, Nora tried to quell the roiling anxiety in her stomach. In her arms, her son slept peacefully, completely unaware of the upheaval taking place around him.

When they touched down on a sprawling property on the beachfront outside of town, she watched as Duarte set about ordering his guards to secure the perimeter while he escorted her inside. This reminder of the danger she had been in back at his villa made her begin to tremble all over again.

She knew that Duarte's protection was the safest thing for her and Liam right now, but it was only a matter of time before he figured out that she was hiding far more than just her brief relationship with him.

Nora barely registered her surroundings as he showed her to the large master suite of the house, explaining that his cousin and her husband lived on this historically preserved property year-round, in a separate groundskeeper's cottage, and sometimes gave guided tours to tourists. He quickly added that the house would be secured and closed for their use for the duration of their stay.

Nora eyed the sumptuously inviting pillows on the large four-poster bed and felt all the tiredness and exhaustion of a sleepless night hit her.

'Get some sleep.' Duarte followed her gaze

to the bed, his eyes darkening for a moment before he exited the double doors of the suite and left her alone.

Nora felt raw inside, as though all her emotions had been swept up into a swirling storm within her. Liam still slept soundlessly, his cherubic face so serene and innocent she felt her throat tighten with emotion.

She was fast beginning to entertain the idea that Duarte wasn't as cruel and ruthless as he'd shown himself to be all those months ago. She thought back to that night in her father's home, when she had arrived to overhear them together, using her as a pawn in the game they'd played.

Her father had told her that Duarte had been playing her all along. That his interest in her had been an attempt at getting inside information on the organisation.

Nora had refused to believe it. She'd fallen in love with a kind-hearted, creative soul. They'd talked about her dreams of travelling as a freelance architect, once she graduated. They shared a passion for design and he'd promised to take her to Europe, to show her some of the beautiful buildings she'd only ever seen in books. It had been real…or at least she'd thought it had been real.

She'd felt sick as she stood there outside the dining room, listening to her father threatening to have her punished for the affair unless Duarte agreed to marry her. And telling him that a stipulation of the marriage contract would be that the Avelar Foundation signed a certain piece of land over to Novos Lideres.

When Duarte had flatly refused the contract, her father had been furious. He'd revealed his ace in the hole, threatening to have Duarte's jet-setting playboy image ruined by bringing him up on charges of sexual assault. Her own father had told him that he had friends who would enjoy giving Nora some nice big bruises to create photographic evidence, saying that hopefully they wouldn't get too carried away with their task now that they knew their princess had been deflowered.

Nora had almost fainted with terror and disgust.

She had waited for Duarte's outrage, waited for him to swear to defend her from such violence, but the silence had been deafening. Then Duarte had dialled a number on his phone and three police officers had entered. The men had been listening to the entire conversation. He'd smiled and spat that *nothing* would make him marry a mobster's daughter or hand over his land to such a crook.

His parting words had cut through her like a knife.

'If you think your daughter is worth anything to me, you're a bigger fool than she is.'

She lay down in the bed, turning her face into the covers to try to stop the tears that threatened to fall from her eyes. She had always known that her father was a dangerous man, but she'd naively believed herself out of the bounds of his cruelty. Hearing him threaten to use violence against her had been the catalyst she'd needed to begin her plan to escape.

Realising how she had been duped—how she had let herself be duped because she had craved love and attention from her father—had meant she no longer trusted her own judgement when it came to anyone. Especially not men who had a motive to use her for their own gains.

But she was no longer sure about her decision to leave Brazil and hide her son's existence. She wasn't sure about anything. She needed to be sure Duarte was telling the truth before she made herself—and her son—vulnerable.

She fell asleep with the memory of Duarte's lips devouring hers and dreamed of him watching her from the shadows of the bedroom, his amber eyes filled with longing and unrest.

CHAPTER SIX

NORA AWOKE AFTER a few hours of restless sleep with her body still taut with anxiety from the night before. She contemplated a shower, but no sooner had she stood up from the bed and stretched than Liam began to wake and fuss for his morning feed.

She dressed in the first thing she pulled out of her case that wasn't wrinkled—a simple coral sundress that was loose and flowing around her legs. She still hadn't quite figured out how to dress for her new body shape, but there was a more pressing matter at hand: feeding the fussing infant who had begun to let out intermittent squeaks, demanding her attention.

Scraping her hair up into a messy bun, she set out for the kitchen. It had been too dark to see much the night before, so she didn't know what to expect.

A long narrow corridor led from her bedroom to a sweeping mahogany staircase. She paused halfway down and looked up, transfixed by the breathtaking original stonework on the walls and ceilings. She could see where the historic features had been lovingly preserved, creating a perfect balance with modern touches.

The large living area had been extended at some point, with a clever stone pillar holding a modern glass fireplace acting as a transitional centrepiece that reached from floor to ceiling. She shook her head, hardly able to take in every wonderful detail at once.

From her vantage point at one of the full-length windows she could see that the rear of the house was surrounded by a stone terrace. Marble steps led down to an ornamental garden that looked perfectly maintained.

The property was cocooned by tall trees on either side, with just enough space at the front to see the South Atlantic Ocean spread out before them.

It was a home fit for a king—or at least some form of nobility—and sure enough, when the housekeeper, who introduced herself as Inés, spied her and showed her to the long galley kitchen, she was only too happy to give her a brief history lesson, outlining the passage of Casa Jardim from being the home of eighteenth-century Portuguese colonials to its present incarnation, housing three generations of the wealthy Avelar family.

Nora bit her lip, looking down at her infant son in her arms. This was what she was denying him. Not just wealth, but history and heritage.

But that life would mean nothing without safety. She couldn't remember ever being carefree as a child. The shadow of her father and his power had always hung over her and her mother, even when they'd tried to live peacefully in Manaus.

On that long weekend when they'd first met, Duarte had told her of the dangers that came with being an Avelar. He was regularly subjected to threats and scrutiny, requiring security wherever he went. She didn't want that for her son. He deserved to grow up free from fear, free from threat.

Steeling herself, she fed Liam and then settled him to kick his legs in his pram before tucking into the delicious spread of fresh fruit and pastries Inés had laid out on the open terrace.

The gentle clearing of a throat caught her attention, and she turned to find the subject of her dreams standing at the end of the stone steps, his body only partially covered by the white towel slung low on his hips.

Nora felt her mouth go dry and a groan of pure disbelief threatening to escape her throat. Of course he would be in a towel...

'I hope you both slept well?' he asked as he took a seat opposite her and sent a single fleeting look down to where the baby now slept in the shade.

'He doesn't sleep longer than a few hours yet,' Nora answered truthfully. 'The bed was very comfortable though.'

'That must be difficult...losing so much sleep.' Duarte frowned, thanking Inés as she brought him out a fresh cup of steaming hot coffee.

'I have many tricks to make *o menino* sleep.' Inés leaned down to coo at Liam, who had woken and begun to fuss and pull up his legs as if with discomfort. 'May I hold him?'

Nora nodded and bit her lip as the dark-haired woman gathered the baby into her arms and expertly placed him over her arm. 'I call this *macaco em uma árvore*. Monkey in a tree.' She smiled and began to sway from side to side, as though dancing. Liam immediately let out a loud burp and relaxed onto her arm with a dreamy little gurgle.

Once Inés and the baby had moved slightly out of earshot, Nora looked up to see Duarte watching her intensely.

'You are exhausted,' he said.

'I'm a new mother.' She frowned, touching a hand to the hair she'd so carelessly thrown up earlier. 'I don't have time to hide my exhaustion under make-up and smiles just to look presentable for your comfort.'

'*Deus*, I'm not criticising your appearance, Nora.' He shook his head with a mixture of anger and surprise. 'Things must have ended badly between us if you think me such a shallow, callous bastard.'

'I don't want to talk about that right now.' She stiffened.

'I know. You asked for some time and I will give you that.' His eyes were sincere, his mouth a firm unyielding line. 'But, for the record, I don't think you need to *try* to look presentable.

You have the kind of natural beauty that most women would kill for.'

He leaned back in his chair, showcasing the impressive deep brown expanse of his bare torso. Nora felt her gaze linger for longer than necessary, her eyes drinking in the smooth muscles that were so tautly defined in the morning sunlight. It had been so long since she'd felt the heat of his body on hers…

She bit her lip, turning to look out at the ocean in the distance.

'I do have one small stipulation,' he said gently, drawing her attention back to his amber gaze.

Nora felt trepidation shiver deep inside her at the predatory gleam she saw for a brief second before he disguised it.

'For the duration of our stay here I wish for us to have dinner together.' He steepled his hands over that magnificent stomach, his eyes never leaving hers. 'Just good food and conversation—no tricks or forcing the issue of the past or the future.'

Nora narrowed her eyes at him, processing his words slowly and trying to figure out his angle. 'What's in it for you?'

* * *

Duarte fought the urge to smile at the obvious suspicion in her gaze. 'Perhaps I just don't like to eat alone,' he said simply.

'You are a terrible liar.' She pressed her lips together, the faintest glimmer of a smile appearing on her lips before she stopped herself. 'Let me guess—you plan to play the gracious host and wear me down until I agree to give you what you want?'

'I don't need to wear you down.' He took another sip of his coffee. 'I have faith that you are going to do the right thing, and I am determined to make sure you are kept safe.'

'You don't need to be nice to me,' she said uncomfortably. 'You are a busy man and I'm sure you have things to do back in Rio.'

'Of course I do. But those things can be managed from afar. You cannot.'

'You wish to *manage* me?' She narrowed her eyes.

'I wish to get to know you, Nora.'

He heard in his own words a bare honesty that shocked him. He saw her eyes shift away from him uncomfortably, her hands twisting the napkin in her lap as she watched Inés pace with the baby, singing softly.

'Trust me—you don't.'

Her words were barely audible but he caught them. He heard the weight of sadness and hopelessness woven through each syllable and was consumed by the urge to stand up and gather her into his arms. To figure out what on earth had happened between them that could put such a miserable look on her face.

'Will you agree to my terms?' he repeated, knowing she had every right to say no and knowing that he wouldn't push the issue.

Inés walked back towards them and revealed the peacefully sleeping baby in her arms. Nora's face lit up with surprise and gratitude as the older woman settled Liam into his pram.

Duarte peered down at the small bundle wrapped in blankets. The child had grown significantly in the month since leaving the hospital, and yet he was still tiny. He took in the boy's dark colouring and once again thought of the man who had walked away from fatherhood. Anger coiled within him.

Inés's voice penetrated his thoughts, asking Nora if she would like to take a moment to rest or freshen up and offering to sit with the baby in the fresh air of the upstairs balcony.

Nora hesitated, looking towards Duarte for a moment. 'I don't mean to leave you alone in the middle of your breakfast...'

Duarte assured her that he would be working all day and instructed Inés not to take no for an answer. No one should be expected to do everything for an infant without a little help.

She smiled, and the two women began to make their way back into the house. A few footsteps from the door Nora stopped and turned around to face him.

'I'll see you at dinner, then.' Her voice was a little uncertain as she waited for him to nod before she disappeared through the doors.

Duarte tried not to roar at the small victory. He watched her walk away, his gaze lingering for far longer than was proper. He mentally shook himself and tucked into the spread of freshly cut papaya slices and warm bread rolls that had been filled with cheese and pan-fried.

This traditional dish of *pão de queijo* that Inés had prepared was one of his favourites, reminding him of long weekends and summers spent here as a child, when he and his sister would fight over the last piece while their father laughed and their mother scolded.

Every time he thought of his parents he wondered why his memory loss had not wiped away the grief he still felt from their death seven years ago. From the moment he'd set foot inside this, their special family vacation spot, he'd been instantly overcome with memories of when he was a child. Yet for some reason he had no memory of the past year of his life beyond blurred snatches here and there. It made no sense.

Shaking off the frustration, he opened his phone and dialled Angelus Fiero's number for an update. Upon hearing that the two criminal henchmen had escaped and gone straight back to Novos Lideres and Cabo, he clenched his fists on the table.

'Filho da mãe!' he cursed, banging his fists hard against the wood.

He quickly recovered and forced himself to think logically. Those men would never have testified against him anyway; it was a part of the sick code of the Novos Lideres. Men quite literally pledged their life to their *patrao*—their boss. And Lionel Cabo got to sit at the top of the pecking order, watching them all fall like good soldiers.

He wasn't prepared to tell Angelus any details about the woman staying under his protection. He simply said that he was working with a witness who was possibly willing to assist in their case. The older man's voice brightened substantially, and he assured Duarte that witness testimony would be enough to get an arrest warrant at least, but they still needed solid evidence to make the charges stick.

The idea of finally putting Lionel Cabo behind bars for his crimes was immensely satisfying. But what would he do if Nora decided not to do the right thing? What if fear won out over that tiny spark of fury he'd seen in her eyes when he'd told her the depth of the mobster's crimes?

Once she could leave, he wouldn't be able to stop her.

In an ideal world, he'd simply offer her a large sum of money in return for information—but he had a feeling that bribery would only send her running faster. She had seemed uncomfortable with his purchases for her and the baby, continuously offering to repay him.

His father had taught him to follow his instincts in business and he'd honed that skill to a fine art, using it to his advantage in all areas of his life. He needed to stay, to get under her skin and find out what she was holding back and why.

Nora Beckett was proving to be quite a perplexing distraction, but if there was one thing Duarte Avelar relished above all else, it was a challenge.

Nora waited patiently for her distractingly handsome host to disappear back to his busy life, as he had done while they'd been in Rio, but he surprised her by staying put at the villa. Shockingly, he didn't attempt to question her further about her revelations. Nor did he mention their kiss.

He spent most mornings doing laps of the pool at a punishing pace, while she tried to focus on tending to Liam, trying not to catch glimpses of his powerful body slicing through the water, or heading off bare-chested for a jog along the beach. The middle hours of the day were spent working, but she soon found that he was not the kind of man who holed himself up in an office all day in front of a screen. Instead, he took conference calls out on the terrace, as he paced back and forth like a lion in his den, issuing orders and asking questions in more languages than she could count.

He'd taken over the large dining table that overlooked the sea, filling it with complicated blueprints and large heavy books filled with technical information. Sometimes when she woke at night, to pad to the kitchen for milk for Liam, he would still be there, frowning as he fitted together odd-shaped plastic pieces and transferred calculations to technical-looking documents.

His yacht designs, she presumed, remembering how passionately he'd once spoken of his creative projects.

They had eaten dinner together for four nights in a row, and the conversation had been far from boring. He was a deeply intelligent, well-travelled man, and yet he didn't try to make her feel inferior because she didn't know about worldly things due to her sheltered life.

At their first dinner she had briefly mentioned she loved to swim, and the next day she'd found a brand-new powder-blue swim-suit in a package outside her bedroom door.

The next night Duarte had surprised her by showcasing his cooking skills, and had pre-pared a delicious platter of barbecued *picanha*, the meat so tender it had made her moan with delight. Afterwards, Inés had offered to rock Liam to sleep, and Nora had accepted Duarte's offer of a short walk down to the beach.

As she'd stared out at the wide expanse of the ocean, spread out ahead of them, she had found herself confessing to him her dream of travelling, of seeing in real life all the amazing places in her architecture textbooks.

He'd seemed genuinely interested, and im-pressed that she'd completed a degree during such a turbulent time in her life, and he had frowned when she'd revealed that she'd had to abandon all her books back in Rio.

The next day there had been an entire shelf of thick hardbacks installed in the formal study at the back of the house, along with a note from him instructing her not to give up on her dream.

He somehow managed to make her feel on edge and completely at ease all at the same time.

On the sixth day after their arrival, she found

herself sitting outside in the sunshine with Liam peacefully asleep in his pram by her side. When she felt a strange prickle on her neck she turned to see a familiar pair of golden eyes watching her. Quickly he turned away, going back to his work, as though chagrined at being caught looking her way.

Nora bit her bottom lip, wondering if he felt the unbearable chemistry simmering between them just as much as she did.

That evening, Duarte passed a message through Inés that he had to leave for the city. Nora tried not to be hurt by his lack of a good-bye, reminding herself that she was a guest in his home and nothing more. But she had got used to their evenings together and felt silly for being disappointed.

The next morning she awoke, ready for the nurse's daily check-up, and was shocked when the woman reminded her that it was the day of Liam's six-week check-up.

She waited with bated breath until the nurse announced that her son had grown and developed at a typical rate over the past six weeks and congratulated her on a job well done.

Her own check-up was just as detailed, and

ended with another smiling declaration that she had healed perfectly and the pre-eclampsia would have no lasting effects. She watched in silence as they were both officially declared fit for travel, and then gave the nurse a long hug as she bade the woman goodbye for the last time.

Duarte had kept his word and booked her flight, the details for which were printed out and safely stashed in the hidden compartment of her case.

There was nothing to stop her from leaving, she thought sombrely as she stood on the balcony and watched the helicopter recede into the clouds above. And yet she had already decided she would stay.

Her complicated feelings for her son's father had clouded her mind, making it impossible for her to come to a decision about trusting him. But really she knew she had to tell him. Even if he had treated her terribly all those months ago and broken her heart, was that enough of a reason for her to deny him the right to see his own son?

Her body was on edge with tension as she tried over and over to think of the best way to tell him that he was a father. She hadn't outright lied to him about Liam, she told herself as she worried at her lower lip. He had made assumptions which she hadn't corrected, but she hadn't directly fabricated the lie, had she?

As if sensing her turmoil, Inés insisted she take an hour for herself to unwind in the pool. The older woman refused to take no for an answer, so Nora changed into the powder-blue swimsuit, covered her pale skin with sun lotion and spent a delightful half-hour wading from one side of the huge pool to the other, floating on her back and staring up at the cloudless sky.

Taking a moment to lie back on a sun lounger and dry off, she found herself able to take in the details of her surroundings. She was awed by the solitude of this cliffside villa. The nearest neighbour was a five-minute drive away, leaving no man-made sound to disturb her peace, only the wind in the trees and distant rush of the waves on the rocks below.

Inés had been right; she'd needed some time to reconnect with herself. She had almost forgotten she could function outside of the tiny bubble of motherhood.

When she got back to her room she found Inés had already fed Liam and put him down to sleep. Her son was starting to slumber for longer stretches at night now, and it was all down to Inés's magic touch. In the absence of her own mother, Nora felt enormously grateful to have such a caring maternal influence. And Inés had developed quite a bond with her son too—although she often threw strange glances Nora's way and commented that the boy could almost pass for an Avelar, with his defined dimple and dark skin.

Nora only blushed and looked away.

The older woman told her that dinner would be at seven and gave her a stern look, instructing her not to be late. It was already getting dark outside, so she forced her tired body to shower and dress in a simple emerald-green shift dress and flat sandals, not wanting to be rude if Inés had prepared a meal.

Putting the baby monitor into the pocket of her dress, she padded downstairs.

In the short time she'd been gone the net of lights above the terrace had been switched on, and underneath was a small dining table, neatly set up for two. In the distance she could see two bodyguards, doing their nightly sweep of the property. She frowned. If there were two bodyguards, that meant Duarte had returned.

'Welcome, *senhorita*.' A slim waiter appeared, motioning for her to take a seat.

'I don't think this is for me…'

She looked around, half expecting a parade of wealthy socialites to come marching through the house. Instead, she saw Duarte emerge from the dining room, striding towards her as if he'd just stepped off the cover of a fashion magazine. He wore a crisp white shirt, unbuttoned at the neck. His short crop of hair was still damp and glistened in the twinkling lights, as did his eyes as he pinned her with an intense gaze.

'I decided I needed to make up for missing last night.' He smirked.

'You've done all this for me?' She frowned, a knot of anxiety twisting in her stomach as she looked around, seeing a man in full chef's uniform hard at work in the kitchen.

'Not exactly.' Duarte let out a low hum of laughter. 'Chef Nico and his team have applied for the catering contract on the new superyacht I'm designing. I'm seeing if he lives up to the hype.'

'Oh.' She felt her arms relax slightly with relief. The name sounded vaguely familiar—she thought he was a minor Brazilian celebrity. 'They're cooking for you as an audition, then?'

'They are cooking for *us*.' He raised a brow. 'You need to eat, no?'

'Well, yes, but…'

'Inés made me promise to feed you. Besides, I found I rather missed your company last night,' he said softly, guiding her over to a chair. 'Do with that what you will.'

Her eyes widened at his admission and Duarte had to fight himself to look away, to ignore how his heartbeat sped up in his chest and pay attention to the dishes that began arriving in front of him for his judgement.

It turned out that Chef Nico's hype was more than justified. By the time the last of the dishes had been cleared away he had already decided to hire the man.

Nora glanced down at the slim monitor in her pocket every so often, but otherwise seemed to be genuinely enjoying herself, and kept up with his deliberately light tales of the day of manual work he'd completed at one of the Avelar Foundation's newest housing projects. He'd spackled walls and lifted furniture up and down steps all day, thanking his good luck that his body was strong despite his injuries.

It dawned on him that he hadn't had a headache in weeks, and that his mood had become more balanced and predictable—almost like his old self.

They took a small break before dessert, and Nora slipped up to her room to check on her son. When she returned, Duarte suggested they take their drinks to the viewing deck and allow the serving staff to clear away the dishes.

She walked ahead of him, the gentle sway of her hips a naturally sensual sight. He shook off his errant thoughts, realising that while he should be planning his approach to secure her agreement to be a witness against Lionel Cabo, all he could think about was kissing her again.

'I love the view from up here. I can't remember the last time I left the city.' She sighed, taking a long sip of her drink.

'You said you didn't always live in Rio…?' Duarte said, keeping his gaze straight ahead. Still, he couldn't miss the way she visibly stiffened by his side, then forced herself to relax.

'Not always, no. My mother and I moved around a bit.'

'You said she's Irish?'

Nora nodded her head, her fingers twirling around the stem of her glass for a moment.

'Ireland's a beautiful place to live,' Duarte said. 'She moved all the way across the world for her work?'

'Something like that.' Nora cleared her throat. 'You know what that's like, though, I suppose?'

He nodded. 'We moved to England when I was just a boy and I started boarding school not long after. My parents wished for me to be a great scholar.' He laughed, seeing the ice in her gaze shift a little, and congratulated himself on his efforts.

'I wouldn't say their efforts were wasted, considering your success.'

He shrugged, tugging at his collar, which suddenly felt too constricting. He disliked it when others commented on his success—an old habit after the years of torment that had come with being the smartest kid in class. He always tried to be modest, to downplay the ease with which he seemed to accomplish certain tasks.

She seemed to sense his shift in mood and changed the topic to the yacht she'd seen him working on, asking if he was enjoying his work. To his own surprise he answered honestly—perhaps too honestly. He told her of the large-scale launch for their US operation, and the pressures his sister and his business partner had been under with Duarte's sudden reappearance and subsequent return to the company.

He didn't go into the guilt he felt about the pain his twin had endured when she'd thought him dead, or how his best friend had blamed himself for the events leading to their kidnapping.

'It sounds like you're feeling the need to prove yourself and your health by going above and beyond all your previous achievements,' she said quietly, turning to look up at him.

Duarte paused and smiled, shaking his head and sitting back in his chair to survey her.

'Did I say something wrong?' She frowned.

'It's more what you didn't say.' He raised one brow. 'I could have sworn I set out to learn more about *you*, and somehow I end up talking non-stop about myself for ten minutes.'

She moved to take a step away from him, and

to his own surprise he found himself circling his hand gently around her wrist. Her eyes widened with surprise, but she made no move to pull away.

'You said you've missed my company...but you don't know me. Not really,' she said softly, barely audible above the rush of the breeze and the waves around them. 'If you knew all the things that had passed between us...'

He watched as she swallowed hard and moved further away from him. If she was hiding things from him, it was likely she had her reasons. But still, looking down at the small handful of steps that separated them, he found he didn't care about the circumstances. He looked at her and he wanted her as he had never wanted another woman. And if she were to give him the barest hint that she wanted him too he knew all bets would be off. He'd have them both naked and in his bed before they could take another breath, gourmet chef and their dessert be damned.

As if she sensed the intensity of his thoughts, she took a deep breath that seemed to shudder a little on the exhale. 'When you look at me like that I can't think straight.' She shook her head softly. 'Liam turned six weeks old today. The nurse declared us both fit for travel.'

Duarte froze, the news hitting him like a bucket of ice water. He leaned against the handrail, looking out at the ocean. 'Have you made your decision?' he asked.

She closed her eyes, as if some unknown emotion was threatening her composure. It dawned on him that he'd never seen her so undone, so close to tears. She was always so strong.

'Hey…hey…' He wrapped an arm around her. 'Look, I understand that you're afraid.'

'I'm not afraid of being your witness, Duarte.' She pulled away from him. 'But I can't tell you about what happened that night without revealing my part in all of it. Without revealing that *I'm* part of the reason you were there in the first place.'

She reached one hand into her pocket and pulled out a slim black thumb drive, placing it into his hand. 'This contains everything. It's encrypted with some kind of code, but I know it's more than enough to blow Novos Lideres apart for good.'

Duarte felt shock pulse through him as he absorbed her words. 'Explain.'

Her words were dull and emotionless. 'The reason Cabo's men were looking for me is because I was a part of his organisation. I... I worked for him for a while.'

She looked away from him, her lips pressing together in that tell-tale way he could now recognise.

'I was initially tasked with getting information from you that they could use to force you to sign over your land.'

She went quiet again for a moment, her eyes flickering between him and the horizon in the distance.

'But it all went wrong.'

'Clearly.'

He frowned, shocked and horrified at her words, and stared down at the black rectangle that supposedly held all the things he'd been working to find. Could it be true?

'I was already trying to get away by the time you were kidnapped. They held me captive in a different location, to ensure that I didn't go to the police. I got free and I got word to your friend, Angelus Fiero, but by the time I got to where they had you...you had already been shot.'

'Why save me?' he asked, watching her reaction closely. 'Why risk being arrested yourself or punished for your actions?'

'I may have done things I'm not proud of, Duarte, but I'm still human.' She shook her head. 'There was so much blood... But I couldn't risk being seen. I had to leave you there. The next thing I heard was your death announced on the news. And then your poor friend was found alive. I didn't even know he was still in there...'

'He suffered greatly but he is okay now. Physically at least.'

Duarte was silent for a long time, his mind working double-time to process the new information. He'd known she was hiding something, but this was unbelievable.

'Look, I'll get my things packed first thing in the morning and I'll be gone, okay?' She moved towards the door. 'I just want you to know that I am sorry for the part I played. I never meant for any of that to happen.'

'You saved my life. You risked your own life

to save me,' he said softly. 'Did you love me, Nora?'

She shook her head, anger in her eyes. 'Don't make me out to be something I'm not. I'm not the worst of them, but I was still one of them. I still conspired to hurt you. To hurt other people through you.'

'Did you love me?'

He asked the question again, more harshly this time, and watched as her eyes drifted closed. She was consumed with guilt—that much was clear. And he should be furious at her deceit. So why did he have the urge to offer her comfort instead?

He closed the space between them, forcing her chin up so she met his eyes. Twin stormy grey pools of torment reached out to him and pierced him somewhere in the region of his heart.

'Yes...' she whispered, a choked sob escaping her lips. 'Despite everything, I loved you... so much.'

Duarte claimed her lips, swallowing her sadness and her guilt and wishing he could take the burden from her. She had been in a purgatory of her own making for months, believing him dead and believing she had been responsible.

Her hands clutched at his shoulders, pushing slightly, and Duarte froze, fully prepared to stop. He was not the kind of man who needed to force a woman to get his way, no matter how strongly his body had reacted to her touch. But before he could pull back she seemed to make a decision of her own, moving up on her toes and pressing her soft, full lips against his.

CHAPTER SEVEN

SHE HAD KNOWN it would come to this from the moment she'd taken a seat across from him at dinner and looked into his warm, whisky-coloured eyes. It was too much—having him this way but not having him at all. If there had ever been a more perfect torture, she'd like to see it. This man who had stolen her heart and then broken it into a million pieces…he was everything she remembered and more.

His strong muscular arms locked her in place as their mouths moulded together like twin suns re-joined. He was a skilled kisser, and the heat of his mouth on hers was sending delicious shivers down her spine. Nora felt her body sing out the 'Hallelujah Chorus' even as her mind screamed at her to stop. To think of the consequences of her actions.

She was sick of thinking.

She felt brazen and rebellious as she moved her body even closer into the cocoon of his arms, letting her tongue move against his in the sensuous rhythm he had once taught her on a darkened beach.

If she kept her eyes closed she could almost imagine that this moment was entwined with that one. That their lives had never been torn apart by the awful events in between. No. She couldn't think of that. It was just him and her and this glorious fire they created between them when they touched.

'I'd be lying if I said I wasn't hoping for this, but I'm not apologising,' he whispered, his head dipping to kiss a path along her neck.

She gasped as his teeth grazed along the sensitive skin below her ear. His hands slid down her back to cup her behind, holding her against him. She could feel the evidence of his arousal pressing against the fabric of her dress. It would be so easy to lift the fabric and feel him properly...

A long-ago memory of him lifting her legs around his hips and taking her in a public elevator rose to her mind unbidden, heightening her arousal. She had always been like this with him—like a moth to a flame. She'd never reacted at all to any of the men her father had allowed her to date…

The single errant thought of her father was enough for her to get a hold on her rapidly deteriorating rational mind and detangle herself from Duarte, moving a single step away.

'Why do you want me, Duarte?' she asked. 'Even after the things I've revealed, you still kiss me like that and it ties me up in knots.'

He shoved a hand through the short crop of his hair, golden eyes seeming luminous against his dark skin. 'I've tried to ignore my attraction to you, because you have made it more than clear that whatever we had before is over. But every time we're together I'm more drawn to you. You're intelligent, and beautiful, and I find myself thinking of you far more often than I should probably admit. I think you still want me too.'

Nora felt heat and desire prickle across her skin at his words. She didn't know what to say to that.

One half of her was crying out to kiss him again and throw caution to the wind—to take one selfish night of pleasure and deal with the consequences of her lies of omission tomorrow.

The other half told her she needed to tell him everything, not just a half-truth. She was stalling and drip-feeding him all the terrible things in the hope that she might somehow manage to keep him. That they might make it through all her painful revelations with this fragile new beginning still intact.

The idea of tipping him over the edge into the kind of hatred she'd seen on his face once before was more than she could bear.

She closed her eyes, hardly believing the selfishness of her own thoughts. This wasn't just about her. Liam deserved to have his father in his life; he deserved the chance to know him. She had to tell him. She had to rip the sticking plaster off.

She opened her mouth to speak, but a small cry came from the monitor in her pocket. She looked at the screen, then up to Duarte.

'Go,' he said simply.

The cry sounded out again—faint, but enough to tell her she needed to go. It was a divine intervention, of sorts, saving her from her own uncontrollable libido. *Stupid, stupid girl.*

'Nora.'

She turned around and saw he was still standing where she'd left him. The night sky formed an impressive backdrop, making him look even more otherworldly than he already did.

'I have to leave again shortly for the city.' He cleared his throat and adjusted the collar of his shirt, looking up at her. 'Have dinner with me again tomorrow?'

She swallowed hard at the knowledge that she had a twenty-four-hour reprieve. She would figure out how to tell him about Liam. She had to. Nodding and throwing him a tight smile, she practically ran the rest of the way up to her room, her heart hammering in her chest.

Duarte stepped inside the entrance hall of the house and was struck by the utter silence. He'd spent the morning with Angelus, and they'd agreed to send the thumb drive for immediate decoding, finding a source they trusted so the information wouldn't be lost. The rest of his day in Rio had been spent in meetings with the future tenants of his new developments, figuring out what they needed and ensuring he was offering the best fresh start possible for them.

He'd eventually cut his day short and decided to return to the coast early, knowing he wanted to ask Nora more questions but also just wanting to be with her.

Upstairs, he passed the door to Nora's room. It was open. He saw the bed freshly made and the small cot. He entered the room, his gut tightening at how empty it looked. He felt his body poised to run downstairs, to investigate further, when a splashing noise outside caught his attention.

He reached the balcony in a few quick steps, peering down to see a blur of action in the pool. Nora sat at the edge, dipping her tiny infant's toes into the water. As though she felt his presence, she looked up and spotted him. A shy smile crossed her lips and she waved.

Duarte pressed his lips together, hardly able to manage the riot of emotions coursing through him. For that split second he'd believed she'd gone, he'd been ready to rip through the country in search of her. It was madness. He felt as if he was losing what little control he'd gained over himself in the past months. How was it possible to feel calmed by this woman's presence and yet so completely undone?

She had essentially admitted to being part of the syndicate that had tried to kill him. She was a criminal by her own admission. And yet something in him refused to believe that was all she was. He had witnessed her care for her son, her intelligence and heard of her determination to finish her studies.

She was a contradiction. He usually despised things that didn't make sense, and yet he kept moving back to her, time and time again, as if he was a magnet and she was his true north.

Even as he told himself he needed to keep his distance, and regain the upper hand in order to move forward with his investigation, he found himself moving down the stairs and through the house towards the sound of her gentle laughter.

Nora had felt as though she were breaking apart all day as she'd wrestled with her decision and her fear of staying too long here in this wonderful place. She didn't quite know how to accept the calm happiness of being so secure and cared for... Deep down, she knew this kind of life was never meant for someone like her. She knew she couldn't stay for ever. Especially once Duarte knew everything. She wished that everything could just stay the same in their little bubble, but it couldn't.

And then Duarte had come back early from the city, and he had looked down at her in his intense way and she'd felt her heart sing in response.

He'd stayed outside with them for much longer than he ever had before, even offering to hold Liam while she took a short swim. She'd felt her hands shake as she'd passed her precious child into Duarte's arms, trying not to stare at their identical colouring and the same little frown between their brows.

The urge to tell him in that moment that he held his son in his arms had been overwhelming, but Inés had been watching them, and Nora hadn't been prepared to do it in the middle of the day.

Coward, she'd told herself as she'd dived under the water to disguise the tears that had flooded her eyes.

And even now, as she showered and dressed for dinner, her stomach flipped as her mind replayed the image of the two of them together in her mind. Father and son...

She knew she couldn't stay there another moment, knowing she was keeping such a huge thing from him. Duarte was not the man she'd thought he was. He was not like her father. Yes, he would be angry at her deceit, but she didn't believe he would be cruel.

She no longer feared that he would want to take her son from her and she now knew she couldn't keep his son from him. Liam was an Avelar by birth, and no matter how much she wished it to be different she had no hope of competing with the kind of life such a birthright would offer him.

She needed to tell Duarte and hope that they could find a way through this together.

Duarte had taken his time showering and dressing for dinner, his senses heightened. Now he waited in the dining room, listening to the sounds above of Inés and Nora talking as they readied the infant for bed.

He had surprised himself with his interest in the boy, offering to hold him that afternoon out of pure curiosity. And something had tightened in his chest as he'd looked into the small silvery blue eyes so like Nora's. He'd felt something protective and primal that he'd feared examining too closely.

He didn't want to come on too strong, he reminded himself. This was just dinner between two people with a mutual attraction.

When Nora appeared, the sight of her curves encased in jade-green silk stole his breath. She always looked beautiful, but tonight she looked radiant. Her eyes looked wider, outlined with the barest sweep of shadow, and the apples of her cheeks glowed with vitality. Her soft full lips were painted a rose-pink that made his own mouth water at the memory of how she tasted.

'You're really dressed up.' She smiled nervously. 'Have you ordered another chef audition?'

'Not exactly.' His voice sounded a little rough even to his own ears, and he could see the way she looked at him a little uncertainly. He cleared his throat, running a hand along his freshly shaved jaw. 'I thought we could go out tonight—if that's okay? The old town is really not to be missed, and I know a place that makes the best *moqueca de peixe* in the whole of Brazil.'

She smiled, and Duarte felt his chest ease.

Nora felt slightly nervous at leaving the house for the first time, but Inés had practically pushed her out through the door, assuring her that Liam would be fine for a couple of hours.

He had begun sleeping for longer stretches of the night now, she reassured herself, trying to ignore the almost painful tug of anxiety as Duarte's car moved away from the house and along the dirt road.

As though he sensed her anxiety, Duarte began filling the silence with commentary, telling her about the small town of Paraty and its rich history dating back to the time of the gold rush.

The historic centre of town was a bustling labyrinth of pedestrianised cobbled streets, with pretty whitewashed buildings and a surprisingly cosmopolitan array of restaurants. Duarte had booked a table in a small modern-looking eatery near the pier, where the ambience was like stepping into a warm golden cavern.

True to his word, the *moqueca* was the best she'd ever tasted. The traditional fish stew melted in her mouth and was washed down by a local wine. For a dinner with a billionaire, it was surprisingly low-key and cosy. She found herself slowly relaxing as she tried not to think of the words she had rehearsed all day.

All day she had been tortured with anxiety. She didn't want to lose him all over again. She'd made bad choices in her life and allowed herself to be controlled by her father, but she did not believe she was truly bad.

After the last of their food had been cleared, Duarte suggested they take a walk down the stone-walled pier to where he had something he wanted to show her. Nora walked alongside him, keeping her eyes ahead and trying to control the swirl of butterflies flapping around her stomach.

The way he looked at her and listened to her, his curiosity unmarred by the hatred she'd once seen… It was as if she'd been given a true second chance with him—with the Duarte she'd known before his betrayal and all the ugliness with her father.

'It's just down here.' Duarte smiled as he took her hand and led her down one of the narrow wooden walkways of the marina. Small fishing boats bobbed gently on either side, gradually getting bigger and more expensive-looking as they walked further on.

Duarte came to a stop at the end, gesturing to a gigantic dark-painted ship that looked completely out of place amongst the more modern white and grey giants that surrounded it. It had several tall sails and an elegant golden trim. A large painted sign along the side read *O Dançarina. The Dancer.*

'This was the first ship I ever set foot on. My father's pride and joy.' Duarte spoke quietly beside her. 'It's been in storage for seven years... ever since their accident.'

Seven years. Nora closed her eyes briefly. She knew exactly when his parents had died, and felt sadness on his behalf.

Duarte pulled down the gangplank and gestured for her to follow him on board. She'd bet the deck alone was longer than her entire apartment back in Rio. It was polished teak and spotlessly clean, as though it had just come back from a week at sea with its wealthy owners. She half expected staff to be teeming below-deck, ready to offer refreshments and hors d'oeuvres.

'I had it cleaned. It still looks exactly the same.'

Duarte smiled, taking his time as he ran his hands along the wooden handrail that lined the sides. He reached down to a small panel and with one flick of a switch the entire ship was lit up with golden light.

'It's…beautiful…' Nora breathed. 'I always knew that you own a yacht empire, and that you design your own ships, but this is the first time I've seen you on one.'

He laughed, a glorious smile touching his full lips. 'I was thinking I might take her out on the water tomorrow, but for tonight we'll have to make do with a champagne picnic right here in port.'

He poured her a glass from the bottle waiting for them.

'This is…magical…' Nora mused, feeling the bubbles warm her throat as she swallowed. 'Thank you for tonight. For being such a kind host.'

He raised a brow in her direction, leaning forward to sweep a lock of hair from her face. 'I'm not here as your host tonight, Nora. I thought that was pretty clear.'

She blushed, turning her face away from him and feeling warmth spread down her body. When she looked up, she saw the twinkling lights of the marina reflected in his golden eyes. His arms circled her waist, pulling her closer so they stood barely an inch apart.

'I've thought about nothing but kissing you all day,' he purred, his fingers softly sweeping along her cheek and down to cup either side of her neck. 'You almost made me sign half my paperwork with your name.'

'I'm sorry.' She smiled, shivering at the sensation of his touch branding her skin. She felt caged in by his large body and his leonine eyes. Trapped in the most sensual meaning of the word. She'd never felt happier.

'You don't sound sorry,' he growled. 'You sound quite delighted at the thought of me in my office, half mad with lust, hardly able to wait to get back to you.'

'I thought of you too,' she whispered. 'I... I missed you.'

Her voice broke on the words, on their heartbreaking truth. She had missed him so much. She needed to tell him everything—needed to take a leap of faith and believe that he wouldn't punish her—or their son—for her hesitation.

But then his lips were on hers, his hands sweeping down to caress her hips and the small of her back. As she sighed into the kiss, sliding her tongue against his, she felt her control begin to unravel. He pressed himself and his hard length against her and she had to fight not to groan against his mouth. Her body remembered his hands and seemed to heat up on command, until the fire within her threatened to consume her entirely.

As though he suddenly realised he was grinding himself against her, he broke the kiss and pressed his forehead against hers. 'I'm sorry… It's been a while for me. I swear I've never felt so out of control.'

'I know the feeling…' she breathed, her mind a tangle of desire.

He framed her face with his hands and kissed her again, slower and deeper this time. His tongue was her undoing, its slow seductive teasing sending her completely over the edge of reason. She groaned softly, sliding her hand under the edge of his shirt to touch his skin. Having him like this, feeling him under her palms…she was half afraid he would disappear if she blinked.

The truth was like an invisible barrier between them, and here in the golden light, with his eyes on hers, she felt as if she'd been given the cruellest gift. She thought back to all the times she'd wished for just one more night with him. She wanted to take this moment and live in it. To have him, even if it was selfish.

The thought jarred her. Of course it was selfish.

She bit her lower lip, feeling the weight of the moment press down on her like a ten-ton truck. She took a step back from him and the words she knew she needed to say seemed to stick in her throat, choking her.

'We need to stop.' She closed her eyes. 'There are things I promised myself I would tell you tonight, even though I know it could ruin everything between us. But now I'm standing here I have no idea how to begin.'

'Then don't,' he whispered. 'I promised you a night out and that means no serious business. Right now, all I want to do is keep kissing you.'

'You don't mean that,' she breathed. 'You're not thinking with your head.'

'I'm trusting my gut, and my gut is never wrong.' He met her eyes. 'Will these things still be exactly the same tomorrow? Are they time-sensitive?'

Nora breathed in a shaky breath, looking up

into his gold-flecked eyes. 'It will still be the same.'

He leaned down, gently pressing his lips to her temple and pulling her close. 'Being here... being with you...it's the closest I've felt to happiness in a long time. Even long before what happened to me. I was always seeking new thrills, always on the move. I was never actually calm enough to just...*be*. But when I'm with you, I'm actually here. I feel present in a way I've never been able to tolerate or enjoy before. I think we owe it to each other to allow ourselves a moment of happiness, don't you?'

'Just a moment?' Nora breathed, half hoping he would draw the line at tonight.

If he ended it—if he showed her he was the careless billionaire she'd once believed him to be—maybe this would be easier. Because this version of Duarte—the one who spoke of happiness and called her beautiful... It broke her heart to imagine a life without him.

She had never stood a chance of resisting him from the moment he'd swept her off that dance floor all those months ago, she realised. She was hopelessly in love with this man and helplessly careening towards full-on heartbreak once she revealed everything to him. Her heart seemed to ache at the thought, as she imagined him looking at her and seeing the lying, deceitful criminal that she was.

Closing her eyes, she sank against him and kissed him with every ounce of love she possessed in her foolish, foolish heart.

When they were both finally out of breath, and in danger of committing a public indecency offence, Nora took a step back, meeting his eyes steadily, without a single doubt. 'Does this ship have a bed?'

Duarte fought the urge to throw her over his shoulder like a caveman and kick open the doors to the cabins below. He'd never been more grateful for the top-to-toe valet service he'd ordered before he'd arranged for *O Dançarina* to be skippered to Paraty. The ship was freshly cleaned and gleaming, ready to sail and with the cabins made up.

Taking Nora's hand in his, he led her down towards the master cabin, briefly giving her a lightning-fast tour as they passed through the ship. Her eyes sparkled with mirth as he pulled her into the large cabin and laid her down on the giant bed before she even had a moment to take in the sumptuous décor.

He adored *O Dançarina*. The ship was beautiful—one of the most exquisitely restored sailing yachts he'd ever known in his two decades of sailing. But right now nothing compared to the view of Nora spread out on the bed below him, her lips slightly parted and swollen from his kisses.

She reached up, looping her arms around his neck and pulling him down for another deep, languorous kiss. Her hands tangled in his hair, pulling roughly against his scalp and sending shivers down his spine.

'I don't think I can wait another minute,' she breathed, her hands exploring his ribcage, and lower, pulling at his belt.

He allowed her free rein for a moment, before taking hold of both her wrists and clasping them above her head. She gasped, her hips flexing against him with surprise and definite appreciation. His little lioness liked being commanded—he could see it in the darkness of her eyes and feel it in the way her heartbeat pounded.

'I didn't come prepared,' he said, groaning

with sudden realisation of his lack of contraception. 'I wasn't expecting us to…'

Nora bit her lower lip, desire warming her cheeks. 'The nurse has already got me covered in that regard.'

Duarte fought the urge to sink into her then and there with relief. 'Remind me to send that woman a gift basket,' he said, and smiled against her skin. 'I know I'm clean.'

'Thank God,' she breathed.

Her nervous chuckle fast turned into a groan of pleasure as he licked the sensitive skin below her ear and gently bit down.

'I don't know where I want to kiss most,' he murmured, trailing a torturously slow path of kisses along her collarbone. 'The glimpses of you in that bathing suit have played in my memory for so long I could hardly imagine having you in the flesh.'

'You have me,' she breathed. 'I'm not going anywhere.'

Something blazed in her eyes and made his chest feel so tight he had to look away, his mouth seeking out her hardened nipples through the silk material of her dress. He focused on teasing the peak, feeling her gasp and thrust against him, following the delicious friction.

Heat, passion, desire. This he could deal with. Two people using one another for pleasure and release. His sex-starved body seemed to have gone into overdrive, wanting all of her at once. That was the only explanation for the over-whelming feelings coursing through him with each touch.

If he wasn't careful this would all be over be-fore he'd even begun, and he wanted to make this good for her. For both of them. She wanted him just as badly as he wanted her—he could feel it in the gentle flex of her thigh muscles around his shoulders as he moved lower.

Letting go of her wrists, he looked up at her from the valley of her thighs. 'Take off your dress.'

She slid the material over one shoulder, then the other, drawing it down to her waist. Duarte pulled it the rest of the way, biting down on his lower lip as her perfect porcelain skin was revealed to him inch by inch. Her small firm breasts were tipped with rose, the skin leading down to the lush curves of her waist and hips flawless, with only the lightest silver streaks on her hips to give any hint that she'd been swollen with a child six weeks before.

His eyes fell to the thin pink scar at the bottom of her stomach, his fingers reaching out to caress it. She froze, her hands covering her stomach with a grimace. Duarte frowned, lowering his lips to kiss her navel through her fingers, distracting her and easing the tension away until she was molten beneath him once more.

The idea that she might want her to hide her body from him was ridiculous. Did she not see what he saw? She was beautiful. More than beautiful—she was intoxicating.

He remembered that once, a long time ago, he had believed himself to be an accomplished lover, but right now he felt as if he was drunk on her beauty, his senses overwhelmed and uncoordinated.

Using her responses as his map, he slowly found his rhythm again, leaning down to kiss the inside of one knee and moving slowly upwards. His hands held her hips in place and she gyrated against his grip, begging him to move faster. To take her where she wanted to go.

'Please, Duarte,' she breathed, her hands moving down to tangle in his hair once more.

Her words seemed to echo in his mind, and there was something so familiar in them, something so right. He felt as if he had been waiting a lifetime to claim her this way, as if something deep within him craved having her body under his command.

He focused on the slow torture of removing the delicate white silk that was the only barrier left between them. His lips moved slowly along her soft flesh to where a silken thatch of red curls was the last barrier to the heart of her. He knew exactly what she wanted, what she needed, as he set about stroking and kissing her exactly where she needed him most.

Her low, drawn-out moan of pleasure was almost enough to send him over the edge himself. He focused on her, on the erotic breathless sounds she made as she crested towards the release she needed, and prayed that he wouldn't lose himself in such torture.

She looked down at him, meeting his eyes just as she neared the peak.

'Come for me, Nora,' he growled against her, feeling heat pulse in his groin as she followed his command with a brutal arching of her back and a sound that sent him wild.

He was over her in seconds, readying himself at her entrance.

Nora took him into the cradle of her thighs, her heart on the verge of bursting open with pleasure and emotion sweeping through her body. The way he looked down at her as he braced his powerful arms either side of her head… She almost came all over again.

Neither of them spoke as he pressed the tip of himself against her, but his eyes remained focused on her face as he slowly joined them, inch by glorious inch.

She felt a delicious stretch that almost bordered on pain at his more than sizeable girth. She looked away, embarrassed that she was not used to the sensation, and her body seemed to clench momentarily against the invasion.

He frowned, one hand cupping her cheek, forcing her to look up and see the silent question in his golden eyes. She covered his hand with her own, moving slowly against him, testing the sensation and feeling her inner muscles relax and pulse against the heat of him. He followed her lead, withdrawing slowly, then angling himself to move back inside in a slow stroke.

The sudden pulse of electricity that tightened inside her made her gasp, then smile up at him. That was all the encouragement he needed and he slowly moved against her, closing his eyes and letting out a low growl of pure animal pleasure. She moved too, her nails digging into his shoulders as he kept his rhythm slow but firm.

Her body remembered what to do, her hips seeming to arch against him of their own volition, her legs winding around him and pulling him closer. His thrusts became a delicious brutal force against her core, sending her towards a second release.

She didn't think her body could withstand any more pleasure, but she was wrong. This climax felt completely different from the first, so intense she felt a knot in her throat as he looked down at her and twined his fingers through hers. She had the strongest urge to close her eyes against the intimacy of the moment, fearing she might ruin everything by crying. But if this was the last time he would look at her this way, she didn't want to hide.

She watched him move, feeling him grind the pleasure between them higher than she'd even thought possible. Just as her pleasure broke, and she heard an earth-shattering moan escape her own lips, he kissed her. His mouth captured the sound as he shuddered, growling into the kiss as he finally gave in and found his own release.

Nora wished they could have stayed lying side by side on the beautiful antique yacht for hours. The gentle sway of the water beneath them made it feel even more like a dream, but like all fairy-tales the magic had a time limit.

When she reluctantly announced that it was time to get back to the house and relieve Inés of her duties, Duarte agreed, helping her to dress. But his attempts at help quickly turned into another frantic lovemaking session, with her pressed against the stern of the ship, looking out at the lights of the town glittering across the black glass of the Atlantic.

Breathless, and drunk on passion, she smiled for the entire drive back to the house.

Inés was waiting in the kitchen and chuckled knowingly at Nora's rumpled dress, before quickly updating her on Liam's thoroughly uneventful sleep and leaving them alone.

Nora went upstairs, checking on her son and tucking his covers around him. When she turned around, Duarte was in the doorway of the balcony watching her.

She bit her lower lip, feeling the weight of the moment pressing down on her. She walked towards him, and once more the words she knew she needed to say stuck in her throat, choking her. When she finally reached his side, his fingers came up to her lips.

'I see that serious look creeping back in,' he whispered. 'But the night isn't over yet.'

He gathered her up against him, taking her across the balcony and through the doors to his bedroom.

Nora shut off her mind, focusing on showing him the love she felt with every touch of her lips and her body against his.

CHAPTER EIGHT

DUARTE AWOKE TO an empty bed.

Sunlight streamed in through the balcony doors and a single look at the time on his watch had his brows raising. He hadn't slept for this long or this peacefully...*ever*. Not a single nightmare had plagued his sleep and his dreams had been filled with Nora. Vivid depictions of them together that had been so realistic they'd almost seemed real.

He ignored the strain of his own desire against the sheets, showering and dressing in clothing fit for sailing. He had a mountain of emails that needed his attention before the Florida opening, but he felt a deep longing to get out on the waves. He felt an urge to grab his sketchbooks and disappear into his ideas—but, strangely, he didn't want to be alone.

His mind conjured up an image of red curls flowing in the sea breeze and sultry silver eyes watching him as he commanded the ship to move over the waves. No, he didn't want to be alone today. He'd take them all out on *O Dan-çarina* for the afternoon.

His light mood followed him downstairs, where he stopped in the doorway that led out onto the terrace and took in the simple sight of Nora below, dangling her legs in the water of the swimming pool, Liam in her arms. She looked beautiful, her glossy red waves seeming to glow around her face in the mid-morning sunlight.

He was hit with a sudden erotic image of wrapping her hair around his fist as he made love to her from behind—one of the moments in his strange dreams the night before. She'd been different in the dream…her hair shorter. They'd been in the back seat of a car, with mountains all around them. The image had been intense…

As though she sensed him, she turned—and the look on her face was not what he'd expected. She looked miserable.

Something heavy twisted within him as he moved to walk towards her, but the gentle clearing of a throat behind him stopped him in his tracks.

Angelus Fiero stood just inside the archway of the dining room, his expression sombre and agitated.

'Angelus. It's good to see you.'

Duarte tried and failed to keep the annoyance from his voice. For once he hadn't been thinking of his investigation. He hadn't been consumed with revenge. But Duarte shook his hand, dropping the customary two kisses on his cheeks.

His father's oldest friend was a thin man, but today he looked even thinner since the last time Duarte had seen him, a few weeks previously. He leaned heavily on his cane—a recent addition after the gunshot wound that had almost ended him.

'You've always been a terrible liar.' Angelus chuckled, a strange tightness in his gaze. 'I'm sorry to bother you here, with your lovely guest…'

In his peripheral vision Duarte saw Nora stand up next to the pool, Inés at her side, the two women chatting animatedly.

He guided Angelus away from the windows and down the long hall to his barely used study at the back of the house. It was a dark room, lined with dusty bookcases, and it had an air of bleakness about it. He'd always hated the room, even when his father had used it as his study during their long summers here.

He sat on one of the high-backed armchairs and motioned for Angelus to take the other, frowning when the man refused his offer of coffee or any other refreshment.

A tightness settled into his gut.

'I have news.' Angelus snapped open the slim file he carried, a look of mild discomfort on his face. 'The evidence on the thumb drive was... fruitful.'

'Excellent.' Duarte reached for the file, only to have Angelus pull it back, a look of warning in his eyes.

'It involves your parents.'

The older man's eyes shone suspiciously as he glanced away, out of the window, towards the view of the front courtyard beyond. When he finally met his eyes again, they were suspiciously misty.

'Their deaths were not an accident, Duarte.'

The world stopped for a moment.

Duarte felt himself stand up, felt his hand snatch the file from Angelus's fingers. He saw the old man's pained look as though through a fog.

His heartbeat pounded in his ears as he read the detailed report outlining the various anonymous hitmen on Lionel Cabo's payroll and the jobs they'd been paid to complete. One item had been highlighted, dated seven years previously in London, England. Targets: Guilhermo and Rose Avelar.

He closed his eyes against the awful truth, willing it to disappear.

His parents had been good people. His father had been sole heir to his family fortune and had made the difficult decision to risk it all on a better future for his home city. The Avelar Foundation's development projects and charity efforts in Rio were world-famous. To think that their vision and refusal to bow to corruption had led to their deaths, just as it had almost led to his own…

'This was on the thumb drive Nora gave me?' He heard himself speak.

Fiero let out a heaving sigh. 'That's the next thing.' He stood up, his mouth tightening into a line. 'We pulled in a few of Cabo's associates for questioning. It didn't take much for them to start talking once they saw how much evidence we had against them. And they seemed to know exactly who our informant was: the only person Lionel Cabo had ever allowed to leave his organisation alive—the only person who had access to such secure information because she lived under the same roof. Duarte, she's his daughter. He had her identity kept secret, but we found it all.'

Another file was shoved into his hands. Images of countless passports and identities on each page. A couple of arrests under fake names. But there was a name at the top, on an original birth certificate that had been hidden from public record: Eleanora Cabo.

Duarte felt the world tilt on its axis for a moment.

Eleanora Cabo.

That name…

He stared from his old friend to the serious, frowning photograph of the woman he'd just made love to for half the night, feeling shock turn him to stone. 'How can this be?'

'Her mother is an Irish ecologist, currently running a wildlife sanctuary in Manaus. She divorced Lionel Cabo after less than a year of marriage, a divorce most likely linked to severe injuries sustained by her at the hands of a male she refused to name. Her anonymity was part of a legal agreement. As was changing her daughter's name and barring him from all access to her until she was an adult. It seems she reconnected with her father the moment she turned eighteen.'

Duarte felt nausea burn his gut.

Lionel Cabo's daughter.

Cabo. The man who had killed his parents. Who had tried to have him killed.

Disbelief and rage fought within him. His temples throbbed and he rubbed circles against his skin, trying to calm the rising sensation.

A flash of memory struck, the picture in his mind so clear it made him dizzy. He saw himself standing in the grand entrance hall of a house he'd only ever seen before in pictures from his investigations: the Cabo mansion. He was looking down at the woman in front of him, cruel words spilling from his lips.

Nora's hair was shorter, blow-dried into a perfect style. She grabbed his wrist as he walked past her. *'Duarte. Please...don't leave me with him.'*

It was definitely a memory... Dear God!

Suddenly all his vivid dreams made sense. They were *memories*. Memories of the weeks he'd spent falling for a mysterious redhead in Rio, only to have his life become a living nightmare.

He turned away from Angelus's worried face, striding to the window and bracing his hands on the cold marble ledge for support. He crushed his fist against his forehead as more memories came rushing back.

The first time he'd seen her...the way he'd been drawn to her like a moth to a flame across the dance floor in a crowded samba club.

He'd been taken from that first glance. She'd been sexy, yet shy, fiercely intelligent and adventurous. Only having her for stolen hours at a time had been a thrill. She'd been shockingly inexperienced, but eager and honest in her pleasure, and of course he'd risen to the delicious challenge of initiating her into the world of lovemaking in every way he'd been able to think of.

She'd become an obsession. He'd even thought himself halfway in love with her until Cabo had approached him and revealed everything.

It had all made terrible sense. He'd been her mark. She'd been playing the part of his perfect woman.

And when the opportunity had come to play her at her own game he'd taken it—meeting with Lionel Cabo right under her nose and letting him offer his own daughter as a reward, only to throw it back in the man's face.

Angelus's words rang in his ears. *A secret.*

On their last night together they'd fallen asleep and she'd awoken in a panic. He'd had to run after her and convince her to let him drive her home. She'd refused, saying her father was overprotective. Their hours together were stolen because she had to sneak out. She wasn't allowed to leave the house alone.

He'd thought perhaps it was a religious thing, but then he'd found out the truth.

To know that her mother had gone so far as to get a court order against her child's father suggested something more than normal marital discord.

That haunting image of Nora's face in her father's entrance hall replayed in his mind again.

'Please, don't leave me with him.'

The Nora he knew would never beg. Not unless she was desperate. She'd been a prisoner in her own home and he'd left her there. He'd used her just as badly as her own father had done.

The memory of it made him tense with guilt. No, not guilt.

He stood up, fisting his hands through his hair. She'd made a fool of him. She'd had the evidence that could prove her father's guilt all this time. She'd been a guest in his home, eaten meals with him, made love to him, and never once thought to reveal all this. She'd said she'd had that thumb drive for months, that it had been her insurance. Surely that meant she had read it? Had seen his parents' names on that hit list?

He closed his eyes against the thought, the pain in his temples almost unbearable. The resurgence of his buried memories was like being hit in the head with that bullet all over again. He felt unbalanced and nauseated.

'I understand that this is a lot to take in,' said Angelus, sighing and shaking his head solemnly. 'What do you plan to do with her?'

'What do you mean?' Duarte frowned.

'Well, I came here to talk to you first. To

warn you that the police want to move to arrest both Cabo and his daughter immediately.'

'No.' The word emerged as little more than a growl from his lips.

Angelus pursed his lips, eyeing him speculatively. 'She was part of Cabo's mobster family, Duarte. Possibly she knew that your parents were murdered and kept it to herself.'

'She gave me that evidence willingly. Surely that is in her favour?'

'Are you involved with her?'

When Duarte merely scowled, the old man let out a harsh frustrated sigh.

'This could be another part of Cabo's plan. Slithering her in here unnoticed and getting her under your skin. As the saying goes, "The apple doesn't fall far from the tree."'

'Don't talk about her like that.' Duarte bared his teeth, shocking himself.

'She has been lying to you this whole time!'

'When I found her she was just about to give birth, and she is being hunted by men she fears,' Duarte gritted. 'I quickly figured out that she was part of the organisation. Her personal relationship to Cabo is her own business. She's done nothing to me.'

Except lie to me. Such convincing lies.

'She has a child?' Fiero frowned. 'There's nothing about that in there.'

'He was born the day I arrived in Rio.' Duarte stood, running a hand over his scar as his mind processed the information he'd recovered with his memory. 'That's why I've had her under my protection.'

He didn't mention the fact that he'd also kept her here longer because he'd been enjoying her company, slowly courting her. He felt the older man's eyes on him, could practically hear him silently screaming at him not to be such a fool.

'I'm going to need time to process this.'

Angelus nodded and left just as stealthily as he'd arrived, his cane clicking as he departed from the house.

Even when the sound of his car's wheels had long disappeared up the driveway Duarte stood frozen at his desk, his mind going over and over all the information and wondering what it was about it that felt so wrong.

Nora had just finished settling Liam for his morning nap and now stood frozen on the staircase as she watched Angelus Fiero emerge into the entrance hall at the front of the house. She froze, anxiety stealing her voice.

She'd already been on tenterhooks since slipping back into her own bed in the early hours of that morning. She'd wanted to wake Duarte before she left and just get it over with. Tell him everything. But he'd been sleeping so peacefully, and she'd known her son would wake for his usual feed at dawn, so she'd left.

No matter how hard she'd tried to hold on to the afterglow of their night together, she'd spent the morning with a steadily increasing sense of dread in her gut. And when Inés had told her that Angelus Fiero had arrived, and he and Duarte had disappeared to speak in private, she'd prayed she wasn't too late.

The older man paused for a split second when he saw her, and then looked back towards the open door of Duarte's study down the hall. When he spoke, his voice was low.

'Finally I get to meet our selfless informant.' He narrowed his eyes at her, not with cruelty but not entirely kindly either. 'Surely you must have known that giving us that information would reveal your identity… Eleanora?'

She heard her birth name and something

within her shattered. He knew. That meant Duarte knew. She'd waited too long to tell him and now…

The older man must have seen something in her face because he shook his head sadly. 'Just so you know, I came here expecting to leave with you in a police car.'

Nora felt cold fear sink into her bones, freezing her where she stood on the last step of the marble staircase.

'But you can relax. Apparently you planned your seduction well. Clever girl.' Angelus Fiero tutted, brushing invisible dust from his lapel. 'He's a better man than most.'

'I did not plan for any of this,' she said. She heard the steel in her voice and wondered how on earth she'd managed it when her legs felt like jelly beneath her.

The older man raised one brow, surprised. 'It doesn't matter. The situation remains the same. Goodbye, Senhorita Cabo.'

Angelus Fiero's voice had been a thin rasp in the echoing entrance hall, and the weight of his words remained in the air long after his car had disappeared down the driveway. She wanted to scream after him that it was not her name. It had not been her name for eighteen years of her life. She might have been a naïve teenager when she had been drawn into her father's world, but she had never taken his name.

She took a few shaky steps towards the study, where her reckoning awaited her. She hesitated, and braced her hand on the wall for support as she fought to compose herself. She was angry at herself—at her own cowardice and selfishness. And angry at the history she and Duarte had shared and how they seemed destined to hurt one another over and over again.

She stood in the doorway of the study and took in the silhouette of Duarte's powerful frame against the light from the window. He faced away from her, both hands braced on the ledge as he stared out into nothingness.

She wasn't sure how long she stood in silence, just listening to the sound of her own heartbeat in her ears. But eventually she must have made some barely perceptible sound because he spoke, still with his back turned to her.

'I assume you met Angelus Fiero on your way here?'

His words were a slash of sound in the painful silence, devoid of any emotion or the kindness she'd come to know from him.

'Yes.'

Nora fought not to launch into her own defence—fought to give him time to speak. She let her eyes roam over him, already mourning the feeling of being in his arms. He wore sand-coloured chinos and a navy polo shirt—sailing clothes, she thought with a pang of remorse. He'd told her he planned to take them all out on *O Dançerina*...

Without warning, Duarte turned to face her, then leaned back against the window ledge and folded his arms over the wide muscled expanse of his chest as he surveyed her. Nora felt as if all the air had been sucked from her chest. The look in his eyes was a mirror image of that day in Rio, when he had walked past her in her father's entrance hall. It was like a cruel joke, having to relive one of the most painful moments of her life.

'Nothing to say?' he prompted, his voice cold as ice.

'I wanted to tell you. Once I was sure you wouldn't turn me in to the police...' She inhaled deeply, biting her bottom lip hard to stop her voice from shaking. 'I promised myself I would tell you yesterday, but then you were so wonderful. I couldn't find the right words...the right moment. I was a coward.'

'Yes. You were.' He met her eyes for the first time, assessing her. 'Did you know about your father's connection to my parents' death?'

She felt her blood run cold. 'What do you mean?'

'He ordered their murder. Staged it to look like an accident.'

He slid a file across the desk between them and she saw the brief flash of pain on his face as he spoke the words. She felt them hit her somewhere squarely in her solar plexus. She picked up the file with shaking hands, noticing the highlighted dates and names, reading that further investigations by the police detective in charge of the case had shown the report to be true.

Each line brought to her a sense of horror she'd never felt, and her stomach seemed to join in, lurching painfully. 'I think I'm going to be sick,' she breathed, dropping the file to the floor and seeing the pages scatter in a blur of motion.

She heard Duarte move around the desk to her side, touching her elbow briefly to guide her into one of the armchairs beside the tall bookcases that lined the room. Nora took a deep breath, then another, until finally the nausea and dizziness passed.

When she looked up again he stood at the bookcase, watching her intently. 'I swear I didn't know.' She shook her head, fresh hatred burning within her for the man who had caused so many people pain. 'I hope he rots in hell.'

Duarte looked away from her. 'I plan to ensure he never sees another day of freedom for the rest of his miserable life.'

'Prison is too good for him.'

'And what about you?' He looked down at her. 'You handed me that thumb drive, knowing it held evidence that could put you away too.'

'I hoped you would understand. I chose to… to trust you.'

'Listen to yourself.' He raised his voice. '*You* chose to trust *me*? I have never lied to you once. I have given you nothing but time and patience.'

Nora felt his eyes on her, felt the question in his words, but her shame and regret was too much. She closed her eyes and pressed a hand across the frantic beating of her own heart, trying to gather her remaining strength and get through this.

When she opened her eyes, he had moved closer. She bit her lower lip, seeing the distaste in his gaze. Then took a deep breath, knowing the moment had come for her to give him the truth he deserved. She only prayed she would be able to take his reaction.

'Your parents were being honoured posthumously in the Dia da Patria festivities. You came to Rio to accept their honour. I was sent to find you—to get information from you that my father could use against you for blackmail, to make you sign over that land.'

She placed her hands on her knees, avoiding his face, but she heard his swift intake of breath.

'We danced, flirted, then we walked along the beach and talked. You told me many things I could have used against you. About your sister, about your plans for the future. You were as shocked as I was that you'd given so much away. After our first kiss, I decided to defy my father and pretend my recording equipment had failed. I liked you. I said I was going to the bathroom and disappeared. But the next day you found me at school. I'd mentioned where I went to college and you wanted to return my coat...'

She shivered, remembering the sheepish look on his face when she'd emerged from her lecture to see him leaning against the bonnet of his sportscar, her classmates gawking at such a beautiful specimen of a man.

'But that's not the end of it,' he prompted. 'I remember...more.'

'There was more. You stayed in town for a week and we became...intimate. You returned a few days later and we continued our affair. It carried on like that for a month—until my father found out what was going on.'

'He threatened to hurt you...' Duarte spoke slowly.

'He threatened me in order to force your hand but you walked away. He was bluffing.'

'But my passport records show I took one more trip to Brazil, two months after that.'

'You tracked me down again, all anger and imperiousness. Still, we never could keep our hands off each other for long. I walked away from you that time. Only…we didn't use protection.'

Nora watched the realisation enter his eyes, moving into shock and narrowing to a deathly glimmer. He swallowed a few times, his voice seeming to fail him before he spoke.

'Are you telling me… Liam…?' His voice was a rasped whisper.

'I didn't want to lie to you,' she breathed, feeling her throat catch.

She had no idea how to make him see why she'd waited. To tell him if she could have gone back in time she'd have told him the moment he'd appeared on that street in the rain. But now it was such a mess…

The space between them seemed to shorten and the room felt too small. It felt as if minutes of silence passed as they simply looked at one another, Nora still frantically trying to voice the truth she waited to give him.

'You are sure I am his father?' Duarte's question was like a gunshot in the silence.

She closed her eyes against the tears that threatened to fall. She would not cry in front of him. She had done enough crying over Duarte Avelar and all the strange, dangerous turns her life had taken since she'd met him.

She had often wondered how an intelligent woman like her mother had ever allowed herself to be controlled by a wealthy man. Why she had feared him. But now, looking up at the cold golden glint of Duarte's eyes on hers, knowing the sheer power he had at his fingertips, she was afraid.

She felt utterly powerless as she spoke, as if she was putting herself entirely at his mercy. She silently prayed that she wouldn't regret it.

'Yes,' she whispered. 'Liam is your son.'

CHAPTER NINE

DUARTE DIDN'T KNOW how long he remained silent, her words repeating themselves over and over in his mind as he fought to process them.

His son. He had a son.

An infant he had protected from the moment he was born...

He closed his eyes and swallowed hard. When he opened them Nora was staring at him, her large eyes so innocent and filled with sadness. He felt anger burn in his gut.

'Were you ever going to tell me?'

He heard the coldness of his voice and saw the way she flinched as he took a step towards her, but he was past caring. His logical side had been overtaken by pure outrage in the wake of her deceit.

'You don't understand...' She frowned, standing and taking a few steps away from him.

Duarte closed the space between them easily. 'Explain it to me, then.' He loomed over her, seeing her shoulders curve and her face turn a little paler. He heard his voice explode from him in a guttural growl. 'Explain why—even after seeing I was still alive, even after I offered you my protection and proved I was not a danger to you—you still decided to keep the knowledge that Liam was my own child from me?'

'I wanted to tell you from the first moment, but I didn't trust you. I needed to be sure you weren't a danger. You know who my father is—you know what he would do if he knew that not only are you alive but I had also given birth to your *son*. I was protecting us both. Protecting Liam.'

Her voice cracked on the last word—the first genuine loss of control he'd seen in her. She bit down hard on her lower lip, holding back the obvious emotion welling in her eyes.

'My son is my first priority. He didn't ask to be born into a world of danger and constant threat. It's my duty to keep him safe.'

'You think I would allow any harm to come to my own child?' The words felt both strange and right as he spoke them aloud. *His* child. *His* son. 'I deserved to know. All this time we've spent together...'

She looked up at him, her face a mask of barely controlled pain. 'I'm so sorry. I never wanted to hurt you. I think that's why I was delaying the inevitable.'

'That was not your choice to make.'

'It was better than having no choice at all.'

She spoke quietly, but he heard a thin thread of steel as it wound into her voice.

'Duarte, I've handled this poorly, but you need to understand that I was the child of a wealthy man who believed he knew what was best. My mother almost died trying to protect me from my father's enemies. Trying to keep him from taking me away once she decided to leave him. I know all too well what it means to be beholden to a man with power.'

'Don't you *dare* compare me to him.' He breathed hard.

'I'm not.' She shook her head, briefly touching his sleeve. 'You are nothing like my father, and I know that now. But when you came back...' She shook her head and walked away a few steps. 'At the end of our month together, after my father found out about us, and he went to find you. You know he put my safety on the table. Threatened to punish me for defying him with you.'

'He offered you to me like a prize,' Duarte said, the memory as clear as day.

'And you made it quite clear you didn't feel anything for me. You said I was nothing to you.'

Duarte froze, watching her closely. 'Did he hurt you?'

She looked away. 'Not physically. He always preferred emotional torture. I had to watch them take you, Duarte. My father forced me to go to that Avelar Foundation dinner the night of your kidnapping. He made sure I saw them take you. I screamed and I fought, but I was restrained and taken back to my father's house. He locked me up so I couldn't get help.' She wrapped her arms around herself, looking away from him. 'It was there, during that week, that I felt so sick…so tired and so faint. I calculated my dates and realised that I was carrying your child.'

'Did he know?'

'He called a doctor, who confirmed it. He was furious, but then…' Nora shivered, her eyes haunted. 'Then he smiled. He said now he had another thing over you… That night, I knew my father was at an event with his politician friends. I knew my time was limited, so I demanded to be taken to hospital for fluids, because I couldn't keep anything down. At the hospital I managed to slip away from my guards, borrowed a phone and found out where they were keeping you and Valerio. I sent a message to Angelus Fiero, praying he would get there in time. But when I got there you had already been shot.'

'You told me…' Duarte heard himself speak as the dreams he'd had all those months during his recovery finally made sense. 'You told me to live for you both.'

She nodded.

Duarte felt emotion tighten his throat but he pushed it away, turning from her and trying to get a grip on his thoughts, on the memories that swirled around like loose waves, intensifying his aching temples. She sounded as if she was telling the truth, but something within him resisted her words—resisted the belief that she was a victim just like he was.

How could he believe what she said? She had planned to keep this from him; she had lied.

He steeled his voice. 'Does your father know about Liam?'

'When I believed you were dead, I told him I'd lost the baby. I think his guilt over that was the only reason he let me go, let me leave the organisation. I was afraid he would try to use an heir as leverage against your estate, some-how. I kept my pregnancy hidden while I tried my best to finish my final semester, and then I made my plan to leave Rio. You know the rest.'

'I'll need a paternity test.'

He heard himself speak and saw her flinch at the words before she nodded silently, but he didn't care. Not when the memory of how they'd conceived their child was playing in his mind and tying him up in knots.

She had lied to him. She'd had all these mem-ories that he was only now getting back, and still she had been able to pretend they were strangers.

She had believed him to be cruel and controll-ing—perhaps it was time he showed her just how heartless he could be.

'If he's my son...' Duarte felt his jaw tighten

at the words, at the emotions they evoked within him. 'I won't be kept from him, Nora.'

'I know.'

'Your actions say differently. How do I know this isn't some kind of new play from Cabo's organisation? His blood runs in your veins.'

She flinched as though he'd struck her with his words. 'You could trust me.'

He laughed—a harsh, low sound in his throat. 'Like you have trusted *me* so far?'

'Liam has Cabo blood too. Will you hold that over him? Blood is not the making of a person.' Her eyes met his, fire burning in their grey depths.

'How do I know you won't disappear the moment I leave this house? Where did you plan to go?'

'I grew up in Manaus on a small wildlife sanctuary.' She shrugged. 'I didn't like being so secluded then. But I wanted to make a fresh start for Liam somewhere safe, far away from the reach of my father.'

'If I hadn't brought you here…if we hadn't got close…would you ever have told me?'

She pressed her lips together. 'I don't know.'

She met his eyes without hesitation, but he

couldn't hold her gaze. He couldn't look at her without thinking of what she'd planned to do, without imagining her choosing to keep something so important from him.

The thought that she might even have left Brazil with his son made something roar within him. The anger he felt was too much; he needed to get away from here—from her. He felt as if he was walking a razor-thin edge between control and madness.

A small cry sounded from the monitor at her hip and Duarte felt his chest tighten as Nora met his eyes again. He gestured for her to go, turning away from her to pinch the bridge of his nose.

He hesitated for a moment, then found himself following her, unable to stop his feet from moving in the direction of the infant's cries.

The windows of the room were closed, the shutters keeping the heat of the day out. Nora stood there in the dim light, holding the child to her chest as his cries softened. Duarte took a step closer, looking at the tiny face and wondering how he had ever missed it. The child had Nora's wide eyes, but that was where the resemblance ended. Everything else, from the colour of his skin to the dimple in the centre of his chin…

He reached out, touching his pinkie finger to that miniature dimple, and remembered that first moment in the hospital room, when a tiny hand had reached out to grip his finger. He wondered if Liam had sensed that he was safe with his *papai*? Would he have any memory of his first couple of months of uncertainty?

Duarte knew there and then that he didn't need a paternity test to tell him what he felt.

This was his son.

He looked up to see Nora watching him, a suspicious sheen in her silver eyes.

Clearing his throat, he stepped back from the intimacy of the moment. 'The Fort Lauderdale opening is in a few days. I see no reason to delay travelling.' Duarte kept his voice low. 'Be ready to fly in the morning.'

'You want to take us with you?' Nora's voice was calm, but he saw the sudden flash of defiance in her eyes, a bristling at the authority in his tone.

'I don't want to leave either of you anywhere in Brazil while your father is being taken into custody.'

He fought the urge to reach out and touch the child again, to memorise each tiny detail of his face. Something within his chest tightened again, almost painfully.

'I said I would protect you and that has not changed.'

'Okay.' She breathed. 'Duarte, I'm so sorry.'

He pressed his lips together, unable to look at her without feeling that roar within him starting up all over again.

'I have phone calls to make.'

He ignored the pain in her eyes and forced himself to leave the room. To leave behind the sudden need within him for the child who was such an integral part of him. To leave the woman who had made him feel as if he was finally glued back together only to tear him apart all over again.

He kept walking even after he reached the ground floor and went outside, passing the pool and moving down the length of the garden towards the sea. When his feet hit the sand, he left his shoes and shirt by the trees and broke into a run, taking out all his anger and pain on his body and pushing himself to his limits.

* * *

Nora had barely slept all night, and spent the eight-hour flight to Fort Lauderdale on tenter-hooks because of the complete silence of the man by her side.

He seemed flat, somehow, as if all the colour had faded from him. He was helpful, check-ing if there was anything he could do to help with Liam, but there was a tightness to his eyes when he held him.

Eventually she stopped trying to talk at all and quietly watched a movie on her screen while he worked on his computer. The result was that she was practically delirious with tiredness by the time the warm Florida sun kissed her face.

When she saw a private SUV awaiting them on the Tarmac, she inwardly groaned with re-lief. She had never been more grateful for Du-arte's ridiculous wealth, even if every other passenger on their flight did gawk at them as they were guided off the aircraft first.

When their driver finally came to a stop at the marina, she stepped out into the warm, humid air with shaky legs. Fort Lauderdale was very different from Brazil. The air was almost as heavy as the Amazonian climate in Manaus, but without the sounds of nature, and there were people everywhere. Well-dressed, wealthy people, who drove expensive cars and dripped with luxury brands.

She fought the urge to look down at her own three-year-old sandals and well-worn blue jeans.

Duarte pushed the pram across the wooden promenade, oblivious to the hordes of women who followed him with their eyes. He looked effortlessly gorgeous, in simple charcoal-coloured chinos and a silver-grey polo shirt. Even without the expensive watch on his wrist and the designer labels of his clothes, his entire being just screamed wealth.

Now he was turning that devastating smile on a well-dressed woman who introduced herself as one of his employees, and instructing a young man to bring the rest of their things as he confidently strode ahead towards the gigantic ship at the end of the pier.

Onboard the *Sirinetta II* superyacht, the staff jumped to attention around him, greeting Nora with wide smiles and curiosity. She knew that the Avelar family were practically royalty in

Brazil, because of all their charity work, but clearly he was adored among his staff here too.

She avoided their gazes, wondering what they thought of the shabbily dressed woman walking onboard with a man like him.

Duarte took the lead, placing Liam down in a crib that had been set up in one of the cabins and ordering dinner to be served in the spacious dining area. He told her he would go for a swim first—the daily physiotherapy that he needed to keep his injuries at bay.

Nora debated going to lie down in bed herself, exhaustion warring with her need to speak with him alone. But in the end, she poured herself a glass of wine and waited.

He walked into the dining room still wet from his shower, his chest bare and wearing only a low-slung pair of jeans. Nora groaned under her breath.

Over dinner she made an effort to ask him about his company's expansion and how it had come to pass, but his answers were short and clipped, and eventually she let the silence sit between them, the food having lost its flavour.

'Are we done?' he asked roughly, once he'd

finished his meal and excused the staff for the night.

'I thought we might talk,' she said.

'I have no interest in talking with you to-night.' He rubbed a hand over the growth on his face, and there was a coldness in his eyes that made her cringe inwardly.

'Duarte, I know I have made mistakes...' She steeled herself against the flash of anger on his face. 'But I won't be kept on this yacht alone and punished with your silence. I came with you to see if we could try to find common ground.'

'There is only one piece of common ground between us that we've shared without dishonesty.' He sat back in his seat, a cruel twist to his lips as he surveyed her with obvious interest. 'If you're interested in communicating again in that way, I won't protest.'

'Is this your plan?' Nora stood up from the table. 'You're going to toy with me and keep me on edge with every conversation?'

'Only if you beg me to, *querida*.'

Duarte felt himself reacting to the fire in her more than he'd have liked. She was furious, her cheeks turning pink once she'd gathered his meaning.

He could have groaned as she braced her hands on the table and glared down at him.

'Hell would freeze over before I beg you for anything.' She spoke with deliberate sweetness. 'But, please, feel free to continue using my mistakes to avoid admitting your own part in this.'

'What part is that, exactly.'

'You told me you had never felt anything like what we shared in Rio. I was a virgin, and you didn't treat it like something to shy away from. You made me feel like I owned my body and my choices for the first time in my life. And yet when you discovered the truth you discarded me like old trash and discussed my worth over *cachaça* at Lionel Cabo's dining table.'

'You might have been inexperienced, but you were not innocent,' he drawled, leaning back in his chair. 'You are just as wicked as I am—in every way.'

She licked her lower lip, her eyes darkening. He waited for her response, knowing it was cruel to spar with her this way, but helpless to stop.

But she only frowned, turning away from

him with a sigh. 'Stop trying to punish me, Duarte.'

He was behind her in a moment, gripping her wrist and pulling her towards him. He waited for her to move, to bridge the gap between them. Sure enough, her lips sought his without hesitation, giving him permission. He growled low in his throat at the heat of her mouth on his, as if he'd been starving for it. As if it had been months rather than a mere day since he'd last held her.

They both felt it—the current between them that pulsed and demanded attention. He'd hardly been able to concentrate during his swim, with images of the night they'd spent together playing in his mind, torturing him. It infuriated him how much he thought of her, of how she'd felt in his arms. Despite the revelations of the past twenty-four hours, he could concentrate on little else.

He turned her around, pushing her against the wall of the dining room and removing her worn jeans with one ferocious swipe of his hands. He hiked one of her thighs up over his hip, so he could angle himself against her through her underwear. She shivered, her hand reaching up to cup his jaw, a sudden tenderness in her eyes.

He pushed her hand away, grasping her wrist as he deepened the kiss for a long moment and then pulled back. 'If I wanted to punish you I know exactly where I'd start.' He moved his mouth to her neck, nipping softly as his hand moved down to pull the hem of her T-shirt up with a sharp tug. 'And believe me, Nora, you'd beg.'

She froze, placing her hands on his shoulders. 'What are we doing,' she whispered.

'I'm about to take you, hard and fast, against this wall.' He nuzzled her neck.

'I can't do this.' She pushed against him and he pulled away from her instantly. He watched as she pulled at the hem of her T-shirt, studiously avoiding his eyes. 'I can't be this for you…for whatever anger you're feeling. I won't be used.'

'I'm not…'

He struggled to find words, knowing she wasn't wrong. He *was* angry. He was using her body because it was easier to lose himself in his physical attraction to her than it was to look at all the rest of the things he felt when he thought of her betrayal. When he tried to align the Nora he'd come to know in Paraty with the one he'd met all those months ago as part of her father's schemes.

She moved away from him, her eyes filled with sadness, and he let her go, knowing he needed to put some space between them.

He needed to get a handle on himself.

CHAPTER TEN

NORA AWOKE WITH a start, the light streaming through the open curtains showing it was well past dawn. She reached out to the crib by the side of her bed only to find it empty. In a blind panic, she rushed out into the main saloon, only to find it silent.

She looked around, eventually hearing a low snore coming from one of the larger cabins at the end of the corridor. What she found there made her freeze, rooted to the spot, afraid to breathe lest she disturb the unbelievable scene before her.

Duarte lay on his back, one arm flung over his head as he slept on the large bed of the master cabin. Liam lay asleep by his side, in an almost identical pose, safely guarded by a nest of pillows. Nora placed a hand on her chest, feeling as though her heart might break at the beauty and pain of what she was looking at.

She wasn't sure how long she watched, how

long her mind fought between happiness and despair over their uncertain future, but when she looked back to the bed Duarte's eyes were open, watching her. She waited for another flash of anger or reproach, but his face was utterly unreadable.

He rose gently, pressing a finger to his lips and motioning for her to follow him from the cabin.

'I never even heard him cry during the night,' she spoke quickly, once the door was closed between them and the sleeping infant.

'I was still awake when I heard him get restless and I wanted to let you sleep.'

He stretched both arms above his head, unintentionally showcasing his impressively naked torso. The jeans he wore were slung dangerously low on his hips and Nora felt a sudden swift kick of desire so hard she was forced to avert her eyes.

'I didn't expect you to be comfortable with him so soon,' she said without thinking, her rational mind seeming to have gone out of the window at the sight of this gorgeous half-naked man being so caring for a small child.

'I'm full of surprises.' There was no humour in his gaze.

Nora swallowed the lump in her throat, wishing she had a cup of coffee to busy her suddenly trembling hands. Suddenly she was painfully aware of the fact that she wore her comfortable old pyjamas and her hair was likely a tangled mess.

'He'll sleep for a while more, I think.' Duarte handed her the small digital baby monitor. 'I'll order breakfast to be served up on the top deck. I'd like to discuss some things with you.'

She felt her chest tighten at his words and tried not to conjure up every terrible scenario she'd already thought of. Instead, she nodded once. 'I just need to freshen up first. I don't think your fancy staff would appreciate being made to serve me looking like *this*.'

'On the contrary. I find this look to be one of my favourites.'

His eyes swept briefly downwards to take in her worn flannel pyjama bottoms and white tank top before he shrugged one bare shoulder and leaned lazily against the panelled wall of the narrow corridor.

'However, if you need some help showering I will gladly play the kind host.'

Nora's mind showed her an image of him helping her to shower, his hands sliding slowly over her body...

They both seemed frozen in time for a moment, and she wondered if he could hear her heartbeat thundering against her ribs. He waited a breath, then let out a low whistle of amused laughter as he walked away.

'Don't say I didn't offer.'

She went into the cabin she'd claimed for herself and leaned back heavily against the door, exhaling long and hard with frustration. Was this how it would be between them now? Barely veiled anger followed by meaningless flirtation? Would she ever be able to have a conversation with him without remembering everything they'd shared?

They hadn't spoken yet about any plans for the future, but she knew it was coming. She knew Duarte was already analysing every angle and coming up with a plan.

She pulled a crinkled shirt over her head and looked at herself in the mirror. Even with the sleep she'd had, her eyes were still bruised underneath. She looked as exhausted and weak as she felt inside. She knew that if she had any chance of standing her ground with Duarte Avelar and his powerful world, she had to get back in control of herself. The idea that she'd need to dress to fit in with her surroundings chafed, but she knew how these circles worked.

She looked at herself in the mirror, closing her eyes against the dream she'd harboured of a simple life in the quiet peace of her mother's animal sanctuary. A life free of ridiculous rules and unwanted attention. A life free of deception and threats.

The more she thought of her mother's choices, the more she understood. But she was not her mother. She knew what came from hiding your child away from the world. She would not make that same mistake.

Duarte was not going to allow his son to be raised away from the privileged life he led. So she would do well to stop fighting him. She would have to overcome her emotions and put them behind her so that they could find a way to co-exist.

They had to.

She would not fight, but she would still remind him that she was not weak. She was not going to be ordered around, held to ransom under the weight of his unending anger towards her. She would hold her head high and stand her ground. If there was one good thing she'd learned from living under the tyrannical rule of her despicable father it was how to put on a show of strength even when she felt like crumbling inside.

She would not crumble—not for anyone.

Duarte had just sat down at a table on the open-air deck to pour himself a cup of coffee when he heard heels on the steps. His hand froze on its way to his mouth as Nora emerged into the morning sunshine. She carried Liam in one arm and in the other one of the colourful cushioned mats Duarte had ordered. She unrolled the mat in a shaded corner near the seating area and laid the infant down gently. He immediately began kicking his legs.

She looked up and met Duarte's gaze, a polite smile on her lips as she stood to her full height and walked over to the breakfast table.

His eyes devoured the jade-green dress she wore. Her long red hair was twisted into a neat coil at the base of her neck and he spotted the glint of delicate pearl earrings in her ears as she moved towards a seat and glanced back at Liam.

The serving staff arrived just as he moved to pull out her seat and he felt himself annoyed by their presence, by the pomp and glamour of the entire set-up in comparison with the simple days they'd spent at the beach house. Ornate dishes were being set out between them: fresh fruit platters and warm bread rolls, along with perfectly poached eggs in a creamy hollandaise sauce.

He tried not to watch her as she ate, his thoughts going over and over the events of the past few days.

'You wanted to talk.' She interrupted his thoughts, sitting back to dab her mouth delicately with her napkin once they'd both finished.

'My sister and Valerio will be arriving today.' Duarte sat back too, folding his hands on the table in front of him. 'I haven't told them about Liam yet.'

'You want to keep us hidden?' She clasped

her hands together, pursing her lips slightly. 'Until your paternity test comes back?'

'There won't be a test, Nora.' He sat forward, running a hand along the length of his scar. 'I was angry when I said I wanted proof. Anyone with eyes can see that he is my son.'

'Well, that's good, I suppose…' She shrugged.

Duarte felt a flare of annoyance at this change in her. 'You *suppose*?'

'I told you that you are his father, that there is no doubt. But I understand why you wouldn't accept my explanation.' She took the napkin from her lap and folded it delicately beside her plate. 'So—your sister and her fiancé…will they want to meet him today?'

'They will want to meet both of you, I would imagine.'

'Surely there is no need for them to meet *me*.'

Her shoulders immediately became tense, and Duarte fought the urge to stand up and knead her unease away with his hands.

'I disagree. You are my son's mother.' He sat back, pushing away his errant thoughts. 'I had a lot of time to think last night. And I realised a few things. The first one is that I do not want to miss a single moment of my son's life.'

'Duarte, you know that's unreasonable, considering our situation.'

'Is it unreasonable to want to give him the kind of upbringing he's entitled to?' He measured his words, keeping his tone light. 'I have a large empty house in a quiet English village. It's safe, and the area is filled with young families. He would have access to a great education and the freedom to become…whatever he wishes.'

'That sounds wonderful.' She swallowed hard. 'Of course I want all those things for him. But I can't be expected to drop everything and follow your demands.'

'I'm not demanding anything, Nora. I'm offering a solution that I think will suit us both. I'm making a proposal.' He leaned forward, looking at her until she finally met his eyes. 'I realised last night that we don't need to make this difficult. Despite my anger towards you, I still find you intensely attractive. The idea of marriage to you is not unpleasant.'

Her face was a cool unflinching mask. Her words were deathly calm. 'Am I supposed to be flattered by that romantic statement?'

'I don't believe in perfect fairy-tales, and I'm

pretty sure you don't either. That doesn't mean we can't try to be a family together. It's the most logical path.'

'First of all, you have no idea what I believe in or what I want for myself.' She leaned forward slightly, taking a deep breath before her eyes met his. 'And, secondly, are you telling me that you now trust me? That you suddenly forgive me for the things I've done and who my father is?'

Duarte felt her words hit him square in the chest. He hesitated, looking away from her for a moment to try to school his features, and apparently that was all the confirmation she needed.

Her harsh exhalation of breath held the smallest hint of sadness. But he wouldn't lie to her to make her accept his proposal. He wouldn't make promises and say things he didn't mean. He believed she would put their son first and come to realise that this was the best way forward for the three of them. Surely his honesty was better than empty words?

She turned herself away from his gaze. 'Don't do it, Duarte, whatever it is you're about to ask of me...'

'You know exactly what I'm asking.' He reached across the table for her hand.

She pulled it away, closing her eyes. 'And if I say no?'

Her voice was barely a whisper and he heard the fear in it. 'I won't force you, if that's what you're asking me.'

He sat back in his chair, furious at her and at the way she viewed him. He took a moment to compose himself, feeling the urge to reach across the table and haul her into his arms to dispel those shadows from her eyes. He knew he needed to go into this with a cool head, but his logic seemed to go out of the window when it came to this woman, time and time again.

'I cannot abide the idea of splitting my son's life across two countries on opposite sides of the world, Nora.'

'That is not fair…' Her voice broke slightly on the last word.

'I never promised to play fair.'

'Why marriage?'

Nora could feel hurt and anger warring within her at the knowledge that he could be so cold and calculating.

'Do you trust me so little that you think I won't agree to any reasonable terms for co-parenting?'

'Marriage makes sense.'

Duarte took a sip from his coffee mug, as though they were discussing the weather and not the future entwining of their lives.

'From a practical viewpoint, we live on different continents with very different legal systems. It would make my legal rights regarding my son unclear.'

'That's not an answer,' she challenged him. 'Nor was there an actual marriage proposal anywhere in that ridiculous statement.'

He stood up and took a step towards her. 'I grew up with two loving parents and had a very happy childhood. I'm not some eternal bachelor; I always planned to settle down and start my own family someday.'

'What about *my* plans?' she asked, trying to ignore the warm, needy feeling his words stirred up. That yearning she had always harboured to truly belong somewhere, to be a part of a steady, happy home.

To give that kind of life to her son...

It would be so easy to say yes—to become

his wife and commit to live with him, raising their son together. She had a feeling he wasn't suggesting a cold marriage of convenience— he would want her back in his bed—but that was where it would end for him. She would always be the woman who had lied to him. She would always be the daughter of the man who had killed his parents.

She closed her eyes against that painful truth, preparing herself to reason with him as to why marriage was never going to work between them…

The noise of a loud whistling from the marina below jarred them both.

'Duarte Avelar—you'd better not be hiding from me on my own ship.'

The female voice was calling from a distance and Nora felt her brows rise into her hairline.

Duarte cursed under his breath, and a thoroughly apologetic look crossed his features as he raised a hand and motioned for her to stay where she was while he strode across to the top of the steps.

Nora waited a few minutes, trying and failing to hear more than the slight murmur of voices as Duarte stood halfway down the stairs and greeted whoever it was. She moved to check on Liam, scooping him up into her arms and breathing in his comforting baby smell.

When the voices came closer, she turned to see a woman emerging onto the deck. Her hair was a cloud of thick ebony curls, her skin the same dark caramel as Duarte's. Even her golden eyes were a mirror image of the man who stood by her side. Another man followed them, sallow-skinned and blue-eyed.

Nora recognised him from the night of the Avelar Foundation dinner. The night of the kidnapping.

She felt a slight wobble in her legs as Valerio Marchesi looked up at her and narrowed his eyes in a manner that suggested she wasn't the only one who remembered that painful day.

What followed was perhaps the most intense hour of Nora's life, with Daniela Avelar sobbing as she held her nephew for the first time while Valerio and Duarte watched in shock. Apparently the elegant businesswoman had never been a baby person, and nor was she prone to such displays of emotion.

At one point Nora was very aware of the two men speaking in low tones in a corner of the deck. Duarte's friend and business partner seemed to have some things he wanted to say out of earshot. She saw the man's eyes dart to her, filled with evident mistrust, but she tried to pretend it didn't bother her.

When Dani insisted that Nora and baby Liam come to the launch of the new headquarters that evening, she politely declined.

So far Duarte had managed to navigate their entire interaction without once mentioning their relationship status or any details of their history together. She was grateful, but one look in his eyes as he was leaving told her he wasn't finished with their conversation from earlier.

She found herself suddenly intensely grateful that he was a hotshot CEO and his presence at the event was necessary.

When she was finally alone in her luxurious cabin, she lay down on the bed with her son by her side and blew out a long, frustrated breath.

The look on Duarte's face when she had asked him whether he had considered her own plans had spoken volumes. He hadn't even thought of her career dreams, her aspirations. No, he'd weighed up the situation and how it affected him and come up with the perfect solution to fulfil his duty to his son and keep her around as a handy bonus.

Was this what life would be like if she accepted Duarte's proposal? Trailing after him from city to city and waiting around while he attended events? Or, worse, would she be forced to play the dutiful wife on his arm?

He'd said he had a home in the English countryside and he'd made it sound idyllic. But the reality was he was a global businessman; his success took him to every corner of the world and she didn't expect that would change.

The last time Duarte had seen the Fort Lauderdale headquarters of Velamar International, the entire building had been mid-construction. Now he stepped into the glass-walled lobby and was awestruck at the level of detail everywhere he looked.

One detail caught him by surprise. The wall of the corridor that led to the common areas, where the drinks were to be served, was lined with picture frames. Upon first glance, he almost just walked by them, but something caught his eye.

He stopped and took a step back, frozen at

the sight of his own blueprints and sketches for the original *Sirinetta* superyacht. For a moment Duarte wondered if they had been framed and put on show in memoriam—if perhaps he should avoid looking too close lest he should be met with an epithet of some sort about his tragic demise. But there was no mention of his death, only a succinct note on each frame, giving the date of his first concept and each stage on the road to production.

'We wouldn't be here without your brilliant mind.' Valerio appeared by his side, sliding a glass of champagne into his hands. 'You have always been the brains.'

'The creative brains, perhaps.' Duarte raised his glass in toast and gestured to the amazing building around them. 'But you were the one to come up with this crazy venture and build it into the powerhouse it is today.'

'I can't take the credit for any of this particular venture. Your sister did most of the legwork.'

Valerio smiled and raised his glass to where Dani now stood, welcoming their guests into the large conference area at the end of the corridor. She walked towards them, beaming.

'I still can't get used to seeing you together,' she said, and smiled as Valerio wrapped his arm around her waist and looked down at her with obvious adoration.

'I could say the same.' Duarte smiled too, noting their mild shock at his light words as they all began making their way towards the party.

Dani moved away to talk with some of their investors, and Duarte saw his best friend staring at him in silent question.

'What I mean is, it's strangely normal to see you this way. It's like it was always going to come to this.' He placed a hand on his friend's shoulder. 'You make her happy.'

'She is everything to me.' Valerio spoke with gruff sincerity. 'Once I accepted that, everything else just followed. I knew it might cause a strain between us, but I hoped you would understand eventually.'

'I was a bastard when I first came home.' Duarte shook his head. 'I'm sorry.'

'You're not a bastard.' Valerio laughed as they entered the fray. 'You're just brutally stubborn and despise change in all its forms.'

Valerio's words were repeated in his mind

long after they had finished their private conversation and separated to move through the crowd. He *did* despise change; he always had. It made him irritable and hostile. And when he looked at the past few months of his life he realised it had been one brutal change after another. He'd felt completely drained of mental energy.

Except at the beach house in Paraty he hadn't felt drained. He'd felt calmer and more at ease than he had in years. Now, surrounded by a mix of elite international business associates and clientele, he felt wound up and stifled. But he knew his role—knew what was expected of him.

He smiled and shook hands and tried to pretend he cared, when really he wasn't sure why he'd ever cared for this world at all.

The ship was quiet when Duarte arrived back from the event. Most of the staff had finished for the day, in anticipation of an early start preparing for the glamorous party on board the next afternoon to mark the opening of their new routes.

He wandered along the rows of empty tables

on the entertaining deck, surrounded by stacks of chairs and boxes of decorations. In his old life he would have stayed to the end of the party at the new headquarters and ensured there was an after party in a fancy hotel penthouse, where everyone would have gone wild and he'd have ended the night with a beautiful woman in his bed.

The thought of it now made his blood run cold. He'd barely managed to stay for a full two hours tonight—only until his disaster of a speech had been given and he'd been able to slip away.

He was so distracted as he made his way down to the private saloon that separated the guest cabins that he almost missed the subtle clearing of a throat. Nora sat cross-legged on a sofa, her hair once again loose and flowing over one shoulder. She wore her ridiculous pyjama pants and tiny tank top, and one of her giant architecture books was splayed across her lap.

She looked like *heaven*…

He would be content to just lie down alongside her and sink into her warmth while she continued to read and ignored him.

He shook his head to clear the ridiculous thought. If she evoked such intense feelings in him it was just because he was stressed and irritated after his first evening of being 'on' as CEO of Velamar for the first time in months.

'You're still awake,' he said, trying to mask his inner turmoil with a light tone.

'I was waiting for you.' She stood up, folding her arms across her chest. 'I assume you got the message from Angelus Fiero?'

Duarte shook his head. 'I haven't received anything.'

She frowned, picking up an unsealed brown envelope from the coffee table and extending it towards him. 'It arrived an hour ago by courier. It was addressed to both of us. I assumed he must have already spoken with you.'

Duarte shook out the contents and read through the police reports quickly. Angelus had worked quickly, and a warrant for Cabo's arrest had been issued within hours of his leaving Duarte's study. The police had hauled the crime boss out of his Rio mansion in broad daylight and questioned him for hours until he cracked.

He'd confessed to everything, including the false imprisonment of his own daughter and his coercion of her to blackmail and work on his behalf. Nora would be given immunity for supplying evidence.

He looked up at the woman before him, her eyes tight with strain.

'He's going away for this, Nora,' Duarte said gruffly. 'The trial may not happen for a few months, but thanks to your evidence he won't get bail.'

'He's confessed to what he did to me…' She pressed her lips firmly together. 'He didn't have to…there was never any hard evidence.'

Duarte took a step towards her, seeing the way her lips trembled as she shook her head in disbelief. 'It's over, *querida*. He has no power over you any more.'

Nora had dreamt of the day that her father would get the punishment he deserved for all his wrongdoings, but a part of her had always believed him when he said he was untouchable. Now, seeing the cold, hard evidence of his sorry end in black and white, she came undone.

She let herself break, unable to stop the tears falling or the messy sobs racking her chest. She sobbed with relief for herself and the terror she'd endured under his tyranny, but she also sobbed for Duarte's mother and father, who had never got to see their children's wonderful achievements or to meet their grandson.

Eventually she closed her eyes and felt warm arms envelop her. She didn't pull away and stiffen, even though she knew she should. She accepted his comfort and sank into his chest until she could breathe again, which wasn't for a long while.

He didn't complain. He simply held her, his face on the top of her head so she could feel his breath against her hair. When she had finally quietened down, he pulled back just enough to look down at her.

'You are more than just his daughter, Nora,' he said gruffly. 'I was wrong to say that to you…to compare you to him. I'm sorry.'

She nodded, taking a step backwards out of his arms. 'It's okay.'

He seemed almost to extend an arm towards her, as though he wished to pull her back, before thinking better of the movement. 'It's not okay. I know I can be harsh and judgemental. I've done it before to my sister and my best friend and now to you.'

Nora looked down as his index finger and thumb circled her wrist and his hand slid down to entwine with hers. She shivered at the contact, tightening her hold on him and feeling her body sway towards his.

CHAPTER ELEVEN

'I've WANTED TO kiss you all day,' he said quietly.

His golden eyes were filled with such sombre sincerity that she felt her throat catch as his lips gently brushed hers.

'I've thought of nothing else…'

She felt herself fight against the intimacy of the moment, taking into account her own vulnerable state and the memory of his earlier proposal. But she wanted to kiss him too. She wanted to sink into the comfort of his heat and his strength and harness it, to chase away the shadows that haunted her.

A small part of her cried out to stop, to keep talking about the deep, dark cavern of mistrust that still lay between them. But she shook it off, losing herself in the glorious sensation of his lips devouring hers and his arms holding her so tightly.

When he lifted her up and walked them over

to one of the plush sofas, she lay back and offered herself to him. His eyes darkened with arousal and he wasted no time in removing her pyjama bottoms and running soft kisses along the bare skin of her thighs.

She stopped him as his mouth reached her centre, laying her palm against his cheek as he looked up at her. 'I need you now, Duarte.'

Her voice was a husky whisper and he reacted instantly, pulling himself up over her and covering her with his big body.

The first contact of his bare skin flush against hers was almost too much. She spread her palms over his powerful shoulder muscles and just looked up at him for a long moment. She knew that this was real, not an instrument of anger, control or manipulation. And he felt it too, this intense connection between them. She could see it in his eyes as he slid into her in one sharp thrust, his hand splaying roughly through her hair to hold her in place.

It felt far too intense, locking eyes this way as their bodies began to move in a rhythm that managed to be both frantic and heartbreakingly intimate. Nora felt words in her throat, the need to tell him what she felt. But she closed her eyes, burying her face into his shoulder and focusing on the pleasure he gave her. On the way he touched her, the care he took in ensuring she found her pleasure...

Maybe that was his way of showing love. Even if trust could never truly exist between them, perhaps she could be happy so long as they had beautiful moments like this. Maybe that would be enough for her.

They made love hard and fast, barely able to catch their breath by the time they both fell in a pile of limbs on the carpeted floor. Duarte gathered her against his chest and let out a sigh that she felt deep within herself. A sigh of relief, as if he were coming back into the warmth of home after battling through a freezing storm.

But as she lay in the silent afterglow of their passion the silence crept over them once more and reality flooded back in.

She excused herself to go to the bathroom and stared at her flushed face, wondering how something that felt so wonderful could make her feel so hollow inside afterwards. She closed her eyes, wishing that loving him didn't have to hurt quite this much.

* * *

Duarte had spent the night in her cabin, in her bed, his warm body curled around hers. Despite her sadness, she'd slept well in his arms and had awoken at dawn to find him sitting back on the pillows, feeding their son.

After breakfast, he'd said he needed to run some errands for the day before the event that evening. She'd already told him she wasn't sure about attending the event, using her lack of appropriate clothing as an excuse. But as he'd been about to leave he'd kissed her softly and said he had asked his sister to offer her services to help her get ready.

Nora had not been prepared for Daniela Avelar to arrive an hour later, with a full entourage in tow. Though Daniela had made sure to double-check that her presence was welcome before she'd ushered in the small team of stylists, with racks of dresses and cases of hair and make-up.

Now Nora felt overwhelmed, but excited at the prospect of being pampered for an hour. She had always enjoyed dressing up for her father's events—she just hadn't enjoyed his authority over her appearance.

This wasn't the same, she told herself sternly as she felt her anxiety rising. Duarte had done this *for* her, not *to* her. It was not the same.

Her inner turmoil must have been apparent, because Daniela gave her a moment to collect herself and asked if she could hold Liam. Duarte's sister seemed thoroughly enamoured by the tiny infant, and only reluctantly returned him when Nora said he needed to sleep.

She settled him near the open balcony doors in his crib and immersed herself in looking through the expensive gowns on the racks in the makeshift dressing area that had been set up on the opposite side of the saloon.

'If you don't want to attend the event, you can move to my yacht,' Daniela spoke quietly beside her.

Nora turned to the other woman, noting the question in her golden eyes. 'I wasn't sure if I wanted to attend,' she said, clenching her hands together. 'But now I think I do want to be here for the celebration. I just haven't been very sociable of late.'

'Because of the baby?' Daniela asked.

'Even before that. I've been hiding myself away for a long time. I'm not sure I know how to be the kind of woman who wears gowns like this anymore.' She gave a weak laugh.

Daniela seemed to measure her words for a moment, becoming serious. 'Valerio told me who you are. Who your father is.' Golden eyes met hers earnestly.

Nora stiffened, looking away towards where her son slept. She wondered if Duarte had told his sister what her father had done. Why their beloved parents were no longer alive. She felt shame creep into her, clogging her throat.

Daniela stood up and closed the space between them. 'He also told me that you risked your father's wrath to try to save his life on that terrible night, and most likely saved my own fiancé's skin too.' She reached out to take her hands. 'I want to thank you.'

Nora shook her head, finding herself unable to find the right words to protest at the other woman's gratitude. Clearly Daniela didn't know the full story, because if she did she'd bet that this would be a very different conversation.

'I'm sorry you had to go through all that,' Daniela continued. 'I just want you to know I don't judge you for who your father is.'

Nora pressed her lips together, hearing the

kindness in the woman's words but hating that they had to be said at all. She felt the reminder of her father's influence like a weight in her chest.

'When my brother came back from that place...' Daniela sighed, reaching out to examine one of the dresses on the rack. 'He was like a shell of his former self. I've never felt so helpless. But now here he is with you...with a child.'

'It's a lot to take in,' said Nora, pursing her lips.

'He hasn't said exactly what you are to one another, but I can tell that he's different. He looks more...alive.'

Nora frowned, remembering that this woman had believed her brother dead for six months, just as she had. They had both experienced grief and mourning over him, only to have him reappear in their lives.

'He proposed to me,' Nora blurted out, feeling the sudden urge to confide her turmoil in someone. To try to sort through her own tangled mind.

'Of course he did.' Daniela rolled her eyes. 'I bet he told you it was a practical solution too. I often wonder how a man can manage to run a multi-billion-dollar empire, with all its intricacies, and yet be utterly clueless when it comes to the workings of his own brain.'

'It's a rather complicated situation…' Nora hedged.

'With the Avelar family, it always is.' Daniela laughed. 'But if you do decide to marry him, I would be honoured to have you as my sister-in-law.'

Nora smiled, feeling some of her misery lift a little, despite herself.

Daniela walked over and laid a hand on the crib where Liam slept peacefully, taking a moment to gaze down at her infant nephew. Nora felt her heart swell a little, watching the obvious love this woman already had for a child she'd just met.

And as she sorted through the beautiful gowns, feeling the silk and the embroidered tulle, she wondered… Would it be so bad to be a part of their family?

Nora stood in front of the full-length mirror in her cabin, taking in the wondrous transformation Daniela's styling team had achieved in just a few short hours. Her hair had been swept back from her face and made to sit in graceful waves over one shoulder. Smoky make-up had been expertly applied to enhance the colour of her eyes, and her lips had been painted a perfect nude pink that seemed to make the roses of her cheeks glow.

She'd selected a pale blue strapless gown that accentuated her narrow waist and skimmed over her stomach. The material was a gauzy silk, embroidered with tiny delicate flowers that had glittering diamonds in their centres. She hadn't been quite brave enough to choose anything tight fitted, even though, at only seven weeks post-partum, her body had begun to feel normal again—if perhaps a little wider and less solid. This gown was comfortable, and light enough for the warm Florida evening, and the colour was perfect for her pale complexion.

She'd enjoyed every moment with Daniela, from selecting the colour for the polish on her now perfectly manicured nails to stepping into the expensive diamond-encrusted heels on her feet. For the first time in years she felt ultra-feminine and glamorous and...*happy*.

She had a small smile on her lips when Duarte appeared in the mirror behind her. He was impossibly handsome, in a simple black tuxedo with a pale blue handkerchief tucked into his pocket in exactly the same shade as the dress she wore.

'You look amazing.' He moved behind her, watching her in the mirror as he lowered his lips to press them lightly against her neck. 'But there is just one thing missing.'

Nora watched as he revealed the small black box in his hand and held it in front of her. His eyes flicked up to hers in the mirror as he opened the box to reveal a stunning square-cut diamond ring that sparkled and played in the light.

'Duarte…' she breathed, feeling time slow and then spin around her as she turned to face him.

Her eyes were glued to the ring as he took it from the box and slid it onto the third finger of her left hand. It was stunning. It was the kind of ring any rational woman would dream of… And yet, when he slid it on and released her hand it felt cold and heavy on her finger.

She had told him she needed time. She had asked him to wait. He hadn't answered when she'd asked if he'd considered *her* plans for the future.

When she forced herself to look up at him she saw his eyes glowed with triumph and happiness.

'It fits.' He smiled, pressing a kiss to her fingers.

She forced herself to smile back, not wanting to ruin the moment. They had made love last night and fallen asleep in one another's arms; she knew they had more than just a passing attraction. It was only natural that he would assume he could introduce her as his fiancée, wasn't it?

Unease swirled in her gut, ruining the easy delight she'd felt moments before.

But he was about to celebrate the biggest moment of his career, she rationalised. His sister was here, his best friend and other family members. She didn't want to ruin this night for him, to cause him more pain. She had already hurt him so much with her poor choices in the past. He had said he wanted to be a family...maybe she owed him the chance?

The idea of a night of glamour suddenly seemed less appealing. The prospect of walking onto the entertaining deck on his arm and being introduced as his future wife was more than she could handle. She felt her insides shake, but steeled herself against the panic, telling herself to be grateful. To accept what he was offering and not dwell on what was missing between them.

Like trust…and love…

She closed her eyes and reached up to kiss him, hoping she would be able to get through the rest of the night without losing her composure completely.

Duarte was on edge. Maybe it was the single glass of champagne he'd allowed himself, or maybe it was the effect of having Nora by his side in that showstopping dress with his ring on her finger.

Every man on the yacht had turned to watch her when she'd arrived at the top of the steps. She always glowed with natural beauty, but after the added pampering and styling she bordered on ethereal. And yet no matter how much he'd tried to relax and enjoy the celebrations he knew something wasn't right. On the surface Nora was calm, and gave him reassuring smiles in between shaking hands with the various acquaintances and business associates he introduced her to. But every now and then he caught her looking off into the distance, with the faintest glimmer of unhappiness in her eyes.

Daniela had looked after Liam while Nora was busy getting dressed and was yet to return him to his mother. Duarte met Valerio's eyes across the crowded deck of the yacht and gave him a silent salute, wondering how long it would be before he was gifted with little nephews and nieces of his own.

A flurry of movement nearby caught his eye and he smiled as he saw Valerio's parents and older brother arrive. He gestured to Nora to join him and soon he was embraced in the warmth and smiling faces of people who had been part of his extended family since he was a teenager.

Valerio's mother Renata immediately took Liam in her arms and began crying, and when she saw the ring on Nora's finger the tears started anew. The rest of the Marchesi men were more stoic, clapping him on the back and quietly offering parenting and marriage advice to both Duarte and Valerio.

'He is very like Guilhermo,' said Renata.

She smiled, her face relaxed and serene as she looked down at the infant in her arms. 'His name is fitting...'

'I chose it in memory of Duarte's father,' Nora said quietly. 'He hasn't been christened yet, but his name will be Liam Duarte... Avelar.'

Duarte looked at her, not missing the way she'd hesitated over the last name. He was surprised at this revelation of the connection of Liam's name to his father's. He'd never made it himself. Liam was short for the Irish for William, she'd said on that first day in hospital, what felt like a lifetime ago. Something softened within him, knowing that even then—even when she had been unsure of him—she had chosen to honour his father that way.

'Little boy, you will break hearts,' Dani chimed in from his side, and they all raised their glasses in a toast to the oblivious baby, who promptly fell asleep and was placed in his pram.

'Duarte, you must tell us the story behind this beautiful family who have appeared with you out of the blue!' Valerio's father boomed.

'How did you two meet?' asked his mother.

Renata had directed her question to Nora, who immediately began to worry at her lower lip.

'It's a...a long story...' Nora began uncomfortably.

'We met in a samba club.' Duarte spoke over her and fixed a smile on his face, tightening his grip on Nora's hand as he felt the sudden tension in her body beside him. 'Very stereotypical for Rio, but there it is. I spotted her across the dance floor and whisked her away before any other man could steal her.'

Nora looked up at him, a glimmer of surprise in her eyes.

'Sounds like it was love at first sight,' said Renata, and smiled as she reached out to place a hand on Nora's with a dreamy sigh.

Nora stiffened and recoiled, and Duarte winced as he watched the older woman's eyes flash with confusion.

'Were they with you while you recovered on the Island?' asked Rigo, Valerio's older brother.

'No... Nora was actually busy finishing the final year of her degree in architecture,' Duarte hedged, avoiding the way Nora's gaze had flashed up to him. 'She's hoping to find an internship when we move back to England.'

'Such a long way for you to move...' Renata's face softened as she clearly mistook Nora's hostility for sadness. 'Have you family in Brazil?'

'My mother runs an animal sanctuary in the north, near the Amazon. My father is...is in Rio at the moment.'

Across from him, Duarte saw Valerio and Dani watching with furrowed brows. He felt the need to end the conversation, to take Nora away and protect her from having to talk about what had passed between them.

If they ignored it for long enough, maybe it would become less of a looming presence in their lives. He saw the shadows in her eyes when they were together; he knew they had both said and done things to one another that would be hard to come back from. He hoped someday it would be easier. But right now things were fragile between them, too fresh.

'I look forward to meeting both your parents,' the older woman continued, oblivious to the tension surrounding her. 'I've always considered the twins to be part of our family. Now we have two weddings to look forward to.'

'You won't be meeting my father, unfortunately.' Nora straightened as she spoke, suddenly pulling her hand from Duarte's. 'He's a notorious crime boss who is about to be put in prison for corruption, blackmail and murder.'

Everyone fell silent. Everyone except Dani, who took a deep, whistling intake of breath and as usual did her best to try to lighten the mood. 'Murder too? He was a busy man.'

'Yes, he was.'

Nora's voice was rough with emotion as she looked from Dani to Duarte. She opened her mouth to speak again and Duarte found himself shaking his head, urging her to stop while he swiftly changed the subject.

As he launched into a description of their time in Paraty he felt Nora shrink beside him, the tension rolling off her in waves. After a few minutes she quietly excused herself and turned to move through the crowd away from them.

'Have I said something wrong?' Renata looked to Duarte for assurance. 'She seems upset.'

Duarte cursed under his breath and quickly asked Dani to watch Liam while he followed his runaway fiancée.

He tracked her down to the rear viewing deck of the ship, which was quiet and empty of any guests. She faced away from him, her arms braced on the rail as she looked out into the distance. He stood beside her, taking her chin between his fingertips to turn her face towards him. Tears streaked her cheeks.

'Is this because of your father?' he asked softly. 'I know it must be hard to think of him. To answer questions.'

She pulled her face free of his grip, folding her arms across her chest and shaking her head softly. 'I know who my father is. I've had a lot of practice in what it feels like to be Lionel Cabo's daughter.'

'Then what's wrong?' He frowned.

'You and me. That's what's wrong.' She took a deep breath, wiping the remaining tears from her cheeks before she turned back to face him. 'I can't marry you, Duarte. I can't be a wife you're ashamed of.'

'I'm not ashamed,' he growled.

'You're lying.' She threw the words at him. 'I'm not prepared to skim over the gritty details of my life just to avoid judgement. You can't avoid everyone's questions and hide our history for ever. Your family deserve the truth.'

'I will give it to them...eventually. I want them to get to know you first.'

'You're trying to control everything—to manipulate them into liking me just so they don't show the same bias you did when you found out the truth about me. The first time *and* the second.' She shook her head, turning away from him. 'I may have made mistakes, and I may be the daughter of a crime boss, but I refuse to live another day feeling ashamed and hoping that one day you might truly trust me or love me. I refuse to accept the scraps of your affection.'

'That's what you think of me proposing to you? Trying to create a life with you? That you're getting the scraps?'

'If Liam hadn't been a factor in all of this you never would have considered marrying me...' She spoke quietly, twirling the diamond ring on her finger.

'Of course I would have, eventually.' he said quickly, frowning at her words and at the dark cloud that seemed intent on pulling her away from him. 'In Paraty, I felt the connection between us.'

She shook her head. 'That was before you found out about everything that had passed between us.'

Duarte let out a sharp huff of breath, feeling the situation getting away from him. They were both aware that this marriage was to secure his rights over his son, but he knew that wasn't all. He knew he felt more for her than he allowed himself to admit. But the idea of laying himself bare...

It wasn't something that came easily to him. Not after all they'd been through, and not with the swirl of emotions he felt whenever he thought of how she might have left him.

'I know that what I feel for you is more than you're offering me,' she said sadly. 'When I'm with you, I can't think straight. I think I fell in love with you that first night on the beach in Rio and it terrifies me.'

'You make it sound so terrible.' He looked away and steeled his jaw against her words, against the bloom of pleasure and pain they created in his chest.

'It's unhealthy, Duarte.' She closed her eyes. 'It's like I have an illusion of you but you keep everything real locked away, out of my reach. It's hurting me.'

When he looked back at her she'd slid the ring off her finger. She took his hand and folded the diamond into his palm. 'You said you wouldn't force me.'

'I won't.' He heard himself speak as though from far away. He curled his hands into fists by his sides to stop himself reaching out and making her take back her words.

'I'm sorry, Duarte,' she said quietly, and she walked away, leaving him alone in the darkness of the empty deck with nothing but the sound of the waves lapping against the side of the ship to accompany his turbulent thoughts.

CHAPTER TWELVE

NORA STARED BLANKLY out of the open balcony doors of her cabin and watched as the first glimmers of dawn filtered across the waves. She had barely slept, and her tears had continued to flow long after she'd silently collected Liam and returned to her bedroom to hide for the remainder of the party.

Daniela had come to knock on her door at one point, asking if she needed to talk. She'd remained silent until the woman's footsteps had disappeared back along the passageway, then she'd let the tears continue to fall.

She forced herself to get up when the morning light was bright enough. She grabbed her suitcase and began packing her clothes and Liam's into her small suitcase, inwardly planning what she would say to Duarte when she told him she wanted to leave. She knew she was doing the right thing. She knew she couldn't live the life Duarte was offering her, no matter how much she wished she could.

It would only make her grow to resent him. They would hate each other, and she couldn't raise her son in a home without love and trust. They both deserved more.

A knock on her door startled her. It opened to reveal Duarte, still wearing his trousers and shirt from the night before. His eyes were haunted and grim as he took in the sight of her and the suitcase open on the bed. She held her breath as she waited for him to speak, her heart bursting at the sight of him, with the need to take everything back and fall into his arms.

But she stayed still, her hands still holding the clothes she'd been folding.

'You're leaving.' It was a statement rather than a question.

'I'm going to stay with my mother,' she said firmly, feeling her insides shake. 'She hasn't met Liam yet. After a week or two I'll get in touch and we can discuss how to manage things going forward as co-parents.'

'I'll take you there,' he said quickly, his eyes sliding to where Liam lay kicking his feet. 'I'll have the jet readied by lunch.'

'No,' she said resolutely. 'I meant what I said last night. I can't think straight when I'm here… when I'm with you. I need to do this alone.'

He was quiet for a long moment, his jaw as tight as steel as he ran a hand over the scar on the side of his head. Then he seemed to measure his words, looking at her with a silent question before slipping his gaze away to stare at the open sea behind her.

'If you need anything…' He spoke the words on a low exhalation of breath, as though he had just finished waging a silent battle within himself. 'Promise me you will call.'

She heard the words and knew what it must have taken for him to speak them. He was trusting her to take his son. She felt another pitiful bloom of love for him in that moment, for this broken, scarred man who was giving her such a simple gift and likely didn't even know how much it meant to her. The gift of freedom.

It was the first small moment of trust between them as parents.

'I promise.'

She spoke softly, meaning every syllable. She wouldn't keep Duarte from his son. She would find a way to make this work.

With one final kiss on Liam's forehead, Duarte nodded at her once and left, closing the door softly behind him.

The rain had finally stopped falling when Nora drove her rented Jeep through the gates of the wildlife sanctuary, her eyes strained from hours of concentrating on the dirt road that followed the bank of the Amazon. She took in the familiar sprawling fields and the tidy rows of fruit trees on the hills. To her, this place had always felt like a world of its own—probably because during the eighteen years she'd lived here she'd rarely left.

She'd spent years hating her mother for keeping her here, and the irony was not lost on Nora. She was now returning to beg her mother to let her stay.

Her mother's house was a beautiful wooden structure that fitted in perfectly with the tall trees that surrounded it. The architecture student in her took a moment to appreciate her surroundings, how utterly flawless it was in its design.

Dr Maureen Beckett was a fiercely intelligent woman who could talk for hours about the animals she rescued, studied and reintroduced to the jungle. Yet when it came to her only daughter Nora had always found her mother to be distant and far too heavy-handed with criticism. She was not an unkind woman—quite the opposite—but she was known for her matter-of-fact approach and the fierceness with which she protected the large sprawling animal sanctuary she had founded three decades before.

Nora knocked on the door, readying herself for a reunion she knew would be anything but joyous. Likely there would be shock, and judgement of her situation. There might even be anger or, worse, that same cool detachment her mother had shown the day she'd announced she was leaving to live with her father all those years ago.

But when the door opened her mother took one look at her, and the small baby she carried in her arms, and promptly burst into tears, embracing them both in a hug filled with nothing but love.

Once she was safely inside, Nora finally allowed herself to fall apart, telling her mother everything.

Maureen was silent, one hand cradling her

tiny grandson in her sun-freckled arms as she listened.

When Nora had finally stopped crying her mother took the seat beside her and drew her into her arms too. Just being held as she cried… being allowed the space to *feel* everything and not run away…it seemed to make her feel better and worse all at the same time.

And the thing that finally broke her was her mother revealing the thick envelope that had been delivered there a week before.

Nora's results from university.

She had forgotten that she had given the address of the sanctuary once she'd known she needed to leave.

She opened the envelope with shaking fingers to see that she had passed. She had her degree.

Her tears began all over again, until she thought she might never stop crying.

They talked all night, about all the unspoken things that had stood between them for years. Her mother explained how she'd attempted to follow Nora to Rio, but her father had caught up with her and told her if she ever sent so much as a letter to her daughter she would wake up to her sanctuary in flames. She'd had no choice but to come back and wait, hoping that Nora would get away and come home, even as her absence tore her apart.

Nora felt a fresh wave of love and understanding for this woman who had raised her—along with enormous guilt that she had compared her situation with Duarte to that of her and her mother. Duarte would never threaten to hurt her that way.

She found herself telling her mother everything that had happened between her and Liam's handsome billionaire father, expecting her to be horrified and warn her off.

Instead, her mother was thoughtful for a long moment. Then, 'Do you love him?' she asked.

Nora shook her head sadly. 'I do, but he doesn't love me.'

'Men don't always know how to say what they feel.' Her mother pursed her lips. 'I find his actions are usually the best way to gauge a man's devotion.'

That night Nora lay in bed, listening to the gentle sounds of rain on the roof above her, and thought of Duarte. Had his actions shown that he felt love for her?

Memories of how he'd courted her at the

beach house in Paraty made her insides feel warm. He might not have known the truth about Liam then, but he'd known virtually everything else. And even after her revelation, when he'd been consumed with hurt and anger, he'd still shown her small unconscious gestures of affection—making sure she slept well, ensuring she wasn't uncomfortable around his family. When he'd kissed her, she'd felt love.

She closed her eyes and sent up a silent prayer that she hadn't just made the biggest mistake of her life by walking away from him. She knew she was doing the right thing in taking time alone to figure out what she wanted, but it didn't make being away from Duarte hurt any less.

Birds sang overhead and the smell of moist earth hung in the air from yet another heavy morning rain. As the sun peeked through the clouds the rain turned to a gentle mist over the fields. Nora paced herself, feeling the burn in her shins and silently thanking her mother for lending her the sturdy walking boots she wore. Even in her white cotton T-shirt and cargo shorts she already felt the effects of the heat.

In the week since she'd arrived at the sanctuary she'd fallen easily back into the simple life there. Now she reached the office and set about using the computer there to send some more emails, as she had done every day since the first morning she'd woken here.

She already had some offers of internships in London, but one stood out more than the others. It was near to the town where Duarte's home was.

She'd told herself she was tempted to take it for Liam, to make it easier to co-parent. She'd ignored the sound of her foolish heart beating away in the background of her mind. Of course she missed him; she woke up every day and wished he was by her side, but she needed to think practically.

On her way back to the house, she stopped to talk with some of the staff and once again gently avoided the subject of where she'd been and how long she'd be staying. It was a small community, and she wasn't eager to become the local source of gossip.

She took her time, stepping off the track to pick some fresh acai berries. The noise of the animals around her was so loud that she almost missed the sound of car tyres, making their way along the road at a pace much faster than any local would dare to drive. She turned just in time to see a large black Jeep barrel past her, turning at the fork in the track in the direction of her mother's home.

Her berries were scattered on the jungle floor, abandoned as she began to walk and then run in the direction of the house. She reached the fence at the end of the driveway just as a tall, dark man stepped out of the Jeep and turned to face her.

'Duarte,' she breathed, shock clouding her thoughts and rendering her unable to say anything more.

He looked terrible: his eyes were dark-rimmed, his shirt was wrinkled, and the trousers of his suit had mud splatters on them. But even though he looked utterly out of place, she'd never seen anyone look more imperious as he stood to his full height, looking down at her.

She came to a stop a few steps away from him, wrapping her arms around herself to avoid jumping into his arms.

'What are you doing here?'

'Do you want the polite answer or the truth?'

His voice was a low rasp, his eyes haunted as he raked his gaze over her with burning intensity.

'I think we've moved past politeness, don't you?' Nora said quietly.

Duarte nodded, running a hand along the untrimmed growth on his jawline. 'I've been a mess since you left. I told myself I wouldn't try to push you, wouldn't try to force you to come back to me, and I won't.' He closed his eyes and shook his head. 'But I've missed you, Nora. I've missed you both so much it feels like I've lost a limb. I decided that even if I drove all this way and you told me to leave, it would be enough…and I was right. Because seeing you right now, I'm not sorry.'

Nora felt a blush creep up her cheeks at the heat in his gaze. She took a step towards him, like a magnet being pulled towards its true north.

He held out a hand to stop her. 'You said you can't think straight around me, and I know what you mean.' He shook his head. 'I promised myself I wouldn't start throwing my feelings around and negating the very real concerns you had. But we've always had this intense chemistry between us, right from the start. That was never the issue. You were right to leave me. I was… I was the world's biggest fool.'

He took a step away, clearing his throat before he looked back at her and went on.

'I can see now why you wanted to come back to this place.'

His voice was warm, caressing her skin.

'It really is a paradise.'

'I never appreciated it until I left.' She took in a deep fortifying breath. 'But I've figured out a lot of things since I came back. Reconnecting with my mother was easier than I expected.'

'I'm glad you got what you needed.' His voice was rough. 'I took some time to re-evaluate things too. You leaving gave me the push I needed to make some hard choices. I told Dani the truth about our parents. It was a difficult conversation, but necessary. She asked me to pass on a message to you, to say that she misses you and Liam and she will come and find you if you keep her from him for too long.'

Nora felt tears build behind her eyes, thinking of Daniela and her wry sense of humour.

'That must have been hard,' she said softly, turning to face him.

'I'm just sorry I'd avoided it.' Sincerity blazed in his golden eyes. 'I'm sorry for how I handled everything, really.' He bit his lower lip, shaking his head. 'I wanted to tell you in person before word spread that I've resigned as CEO of Velamar.'

Nora gasped. 'Why would you do that?'

'I want to be free to work remotely, with less travel and less of that life in the spotlight, so I can focus on being with Liam. So we can create a parenting plan that considers both our needs and not just mine. Valerio was very understanding; he suggested I become a silent partner so I can focus on my own design firm.'

'That's…that's amazing, Duarte.'

'I don't know if you've thought about where you plan to live…?'

'You're *asking* me?' she said dumbly, hardly believing that he was here, that he was offering her everything she'd never thought possible.

Everything except himself…

Suddenly, his earlier words struck her. 'You said you'd told yourself you wouldn't use your feelings to make me come back. What *are* your feelings, Duarte?'

'Apart from feeling like a fool for letting you go?' He shook his head softly. 'I realised that the anger I felt when I got my memory back was so strong because I was in love with you. I never stopped being in love with you—even when your father came to me, even when I lay on the ground with you holding me and begging me to live. And when I found you again those feelings were always there, drawing me back to you. Back to where I belonged. Once I'd worked past my own stubbornness, and once I'd realised how much I hurt you by telling your father you meant nothing to me, I saw that my anger was only towards myself, and I saw how blind I'd been to what I'd had. And I saw that I'd had the kind of second chance that most people can only dream of...'

Nora felt her breathing become shallow as she took a step towards him, flattening her hands against his chest and feeling the steady beat of his heart under her fingertips.

'I don't want you to jump back into my arms,' he said. 'I know you have every reason to wait and see if I can keep my promises. But if you give me another chance I will do everything right this time. I will show you every ounce of love I possess.'

Nora claimed his lips then, unable to wait another moment to be in the warmth of his embrace. They kissed for what felt like hours, her heart singing with joy at his words, at how his body moulded around hers in a mirror of the relief and longing she felt.

When they finally separated he still held her close and breathed in the scent of her hair. He laughed. 'I think I might have to go back on that promise to leave.'

'I think so.' She smiled. 'I know we have a lot of plans to discuss, but about your proposal—'

He cut across her. 'I was wrong to make that proposal. I wanted to force you to stay with me, to be mine. If we do this now I want you to be with me because you *want* to. I don't care if we never get married, as long as we're together.'

'And if I say I want to live here in the rainforest for ever…?' Nora breathed, keeping her expression deliberately serious.

His eyes widened slightly. 'Well, it would be a hell of a commute, but I would make it work somehow.'

She closed her eyes, laughter bubbling in her chest along with an intense euphoria such as she had never experienced before. 'Well, if that isn't love I don't know what is.'

He lowered his mouth, nipping at her neck with his teeth and making her shiver. 'You are a cruel negotiator, Nora Beckett.'

The kiss that followed was even steamier than the first, leaving both of them out of breath and her shirt wrapped around her waist by the time she had the sense to break away.

'I don't really want to live here,' she said quickly. 'I've spent all week applying for internships in London. I want a fresh start. I want to create a family with you and turn your big house into a home. *Our* home.'

Her hands travelled over his chest, feeling a bump under his shirt. He smiled self-consciously, revealing a chain around his neck and on the end of it…her diamond engagement ring.

'I spent hours that day, picking this out.' He pulled it over his head, placing it in her palm. 'It doesn't need to mean anything. It can just be a symbol.'

'You know, I always dreamt of having my wedding here, in the local chapel, surrounded by the friends of my youth, my mother and our little community.'

Nora held the ring in her palm for a moment, watching it glitter and sparkle in the light. When she finally met his eyes again she felt a wave of emotion so strong it took her breath away. She placed the ring back in his hand.

'I want it to mean something, Duarte. If you'll still have me.'

He needed no further encouragement, getting down on one knee right there in the rain-soaked mud and taking her hand in his.

'I didn't give you a proper proposal the first time and I won't make that mistake again.' He looked up at her, the ring glittering in the light between them. 'Will you marry me?'

'I thought you'd never ask,' she breathed, getting down on her knees with him as he slid the ring onto her finger.

'I never thought I'd be so grateful for almost dying,' he murmured against her lips. 'If that pain was what I needed to go through to bring us back together I'd go through it all again right now, just to have you here in my arms where you belong.'

'Please don't,' she said. 'I was quite looking

forward to celebrating our engagement somewhere private before we're interrupted.'

He laughed, standing up and scooping her
into his arms to carry her into the house in
search of the nearest bed.

'Lead the way, my love.'

'I always will.'

EPILOGUE

AS A YOUNG GIRL, Nora had dreamt of her wedding day. She'd imagined herself walking down the aisle in a flowing gown to the sounds of a classical melody. As an adult, once she'd learned the truth of her parents' history, she'd stopped seeing marriage as something to celebrate. But now, as she walked down the planks at the sanctuary's wooden dock, hand in hand with the man she'd just vowed to love and cherish for ever, she felt her heart swell with joy.

They'd spoken their vows in the old chapel in the village, taking Liam into their arms between them towards the end of the ceremony when he'd begun to fuss. Nora wore a simple white strapless dress, with flowers from her mother's garden woven through her hair. Duarte looked effortlessly handsome in a tux, the shirt collar unbuttoned. She'd chosen the colour scheme, even convincing him to tuck one of her favourite purple orchids into his lapel.

They reached the small speedboat at the end of the dock and Nora turned to her husband, looking over her shoulder at the small crowd of their loved ones, still enjoying the wedding reception and dancing on the bank of the Amazon behind them.

'What is this surprise you've kept so secret?' she murmured against his lips, smiling at the sound of cheers erupting behind them.

'It's not a surprise if I tell you first.' He took her hand, helping her into the boat and getting behind the wheel. 'We'll only be away for a bit.'

She smiled as he manoeuvred them away from the sanctuary and along the river at a gentle speed. She placed her hand over his on the wheel, looking at the matching rings on their fingers and feeling herself smile even wider as the sun danced through the trees.

When he began to slow, she looked around.

'I read about this place a long time ago.' Duarte turned to face her. 'Do you know where we are?'

She shook her head.

'We're at the meeting of the waters. It's where

two separate rivers finally meet and become one after running side by side for miles. Look down.'

He pointed to the river around them and Nora blinked. Sure enough, ahead of them the water seemed to cleave into two different shades. The dark, almost black waters of the Rio Negro ran seamlessly alongside the coffee colour of the Amazon before blending into one behind them.

They stood in silence for a moment, taking in the remarkable feat of nature.

'I can't believe I've never seen this before,' she breathed.

'Today has been perfect.' Duarte turned and took her hands in his, gently sliding her wedding ring from her finger and holding it up to the light. 'But I have one last surprise.'

She frowned, looking down at the inner circle of the ring. A soft gasp escaped her lips. Despite them having barely a week to plan their small civil ceremony, he'd somehow managed to have the platinum band engraved with the date and time of when they'd first met. The moment he'd asked her to dance and she'd lost her heart to him.

'I wanted us to make our own vows here, because I feel like it symbolises everything I love about you. About us.'

'Darkness and light,' Nora murmured, smiling as tears filled her eyes.

'I love you, Nora Avelar.' He slid the ring slowly back onto her finger, his eyes never leaving hers. 'I love everything you have been through, and everything that makes you the woman you are today. I promise to love and honour you for the rest of our lives.'

Her hands shook as she removed Duarte's ring and pressed it gently to her lips. 'There's nowhere else I could imagine making my vows to you than here on the water. This is beyond perfect.'

She slid the ring back onto his finger, smiling as she looked up into his brilliant golden eyes. 'I promise to love and honour you, Duarte Avelar. *Para sempre.*'

'*Para sempre,*' he echoed, sweeping her into his arms to show her just how good for ever could feel.

* * * * *